A true story of a secret plan to take down Hafiz Saeed —
and claim the $10 million bounty on his head.

Amber Sharma

Empty
Canvas
Publishers

Distributed By

Empty Canvas Publishers

4432-36/7, First Floor, Ansari Road, Darya Ganj, New Delhi, 110002

Phone No.- 011-41627043

Mobile No.- +91-9958232447

Price in india : 450/- INR

2nd Edition 2026

First published by Mowgli Productions in June 2025

Printed and bound in India

ISBN : 978-81-965910-7-6

I am grateful to all my sources
without which any of my investigative stories
could not be complete.

Thank you,

Mr. Rajiv Agrawal

Principal - Wilsonia Degree College.

I am grateful to the companions of
Kanha and Bandhavgarh Tiger Reserves
and all my friends.

PREFACE

I embarked on the journey of my life with wildlife conservation, and in the year 2003, I arrived at Kanha National Park in Madhya Pradesh. It was there that I began my foray into wildlife photography, driven by the purpose of contributing to wildlife conservation through my photography.

I firmly believe that pictures have the power to narrate their own tales. Through these images, you can awaken the world's consciousness. Thus, I initiated a photography exhibition with the primary objective of "Conservation Through Photography," wherein the aim was to conserve and protect through the medium of images.

Due to my working style, I began to be addressed by nicknames like "Mowgli" and "Mowgli Baba". During my wildlife photography journey, I learned that wildlife crime is also prevalent, amounting to a yearly business worth 23 billion dollars. This realization sparked my interest in unveiling the realm of wildlife crime. In the year 2009, I established my production house, "Mowgli Productions".

My debut documentary, "In Search of Snow Leopards," directed and produced by me, delved into the world of snow leopards and the Ladakh environment. Through this documentary, I aimed not only to showcase nature's beauty but also to educate and raise awareness about flora and fauna among people worldwide. This transformation led me from being a wildlife photographer to an investigative filmmaker.

As I delved into exposing wildlife crime, I made an attempt to understand the Mumbai mafia as well. I conducted extensive research on the Mumbai mafia, and in 2016, I planned a series titled "Mumbai Mafia

- Unheard Story." However, my investors discouraged me from funding this series at the last moment due to financial losses suffered by one of the investors. As a result, the series came to a halt.

This series was rich in facts and evidence, and I didn't want my hard work to go in vain. Therefore, in 2019, I began a YouTube series titled "Dastaan Kahani Unsuni" , where I narrated the entire story of "Mumbai Mafia - Unheard Story." This series was well-received by the audience. It became the most-watched crime investigative series in Hindi on YouTube. The series garnered over 30,000 hours of watch time every month.

In the year 2016, I conducted a 90-minute interview with Chhota Shakeel, a close associate of Dawood Ibrahim, through a telephone conversation. Alongside this, I had the privilege of receiving interviews from various most-wanted figures connected to the Mumbai mafia such as Ali Budesh, Vijay Shetty, Prasad Pujari, and Ravi Pujari. They would frequently call me, providing their insights, and each time they reached out, my endeavor was to extract as much information as possible from them.

After the COVID-19 pandemic, in 2021, I began gathering information about the attack on Hafiz Saeed, and by March 2022, I had created three episodes on YouTube detailing the planning behind the attack. However, those episodes couldn't encompass all the information. The purpose behind writing this book is to disseminate comprehensive knowledge to the world. In this book, I've documented everything I learned during my investigation. I obtained numerous call recordings and video footage, all of which I've compiled in this book.

Through this book, I aim to provide readers with a fresh perspective on investigative literature. My goal is to enable readers to immerse themselves in every scene of the story. To comprehend each character's speech and thoughts, offering a deeper understanding of their perspectives.

I have written this book in a very simple language. I hope you will enjoy reading it. I look forward to your feedback.

15 Feb 2023

Amber Sharma
(Mowgli Baba)

AUTHOR'S NOTE

"Operation Chachajaan" was first published in Hindi in 2023. I didn't expect the overwhelming response it received. What began as a passion project — a true story that needed to be told — quickly resonated with readers across India. Many reached out to me, urging that this story deserved a global audience. They were right.

At first, I chose to write it in Hindi for a reason. The characters in this story — the men who planned one of the most daring operations to eliminate global terrorist Hafiz Saeed — lived and thought in Hindi. Their conversations, frustrations, strategies, and emotions could only be captured authentically in that language. I wanted to preserve their reality, their intensity, and their raw voice. That's why the original version stayed true to the language they lived in.

But over time, I realized this story isn't just for Hindi readers. It's a story that belongs to the world — a story about courage, secrecy, sacrifice, and the invisible war fought in the shadows. The kind of war that never makes headlines, but changes the course of history.

So, two years after the Hindi release, I've taken the time to carefully translate this book into English — not just word-for-word, but with the same soul and grit the original carried.

And finally, I'll leave you with this: based on the information I've received from credible sources, Hafiz Saeed is no longer alive. But don't expect any confirmation — Pakistan will never accept it.

This book brings you as close as possible to the untold truth.

12 May 2025

Amber Sharma
(Mowgli Baba)

TABLE OF CONTENTS

Chapter 1
MEETINGS

Year 2018

Manama City (Bahrain), Two Afghan individuals visit the Hind Jewelers Gold Shop and meet the cashier sitting at the shop counter.

Afghani: We need to meet Swami ji.

Cashier: Who are you guys?

Afghani: We've come from Baluchistan. We need to meet Swami ji. We are his followers, I swear.

Cashier: Please wait a moment. He'll be here soon.

The Afghani individuals start examining the jewelry on display in the shop showcases and engage in a discussion in the Afghan language.

- Introduction to Swami ji, alias Ali Budesh - Ali Budesh, who had witnessed 60 springs of life, stood around 6 feet tall, had a robust build, a long French-cut white beard, and used a staff for walking due to his age of 60, was a patient of diabetes and high blood pressure. Ali Budesh, an ordinary Arab engaged in the gold business in Bahrain, had a façade that hid a deeper truth. In reality, Ali Budesh was a wanted gangster in India, and his entry into Dubai was restricted. Ali Budesh acquired education in Pune. His mother was Indian and father was from Bahrain, making him a citizen of Bahrain due to his Arab father. His conversations often carried a hint of the Bombay accent. During his youth, Ali Budesh became closely associated with the Mumbai mafia, and his friendship blossomed with Shyam Kishore Girikapatti. Shyam Kishore Girikapatti, known by the alias "Black Scorpion" in the underworld, had started his journey with the D Company. Ali Budesh's strong friendship with Ejaz Pathan is well known. It's a known fact that Ejaz Pathan was an accused in the 1993 Bombay Blasts and he passed away due to illness in JJ Hospital in 2007. Ali Budesh's entry into the Mumbai mafia, his close ties with Shyam Kishore Girikapatti, and his proximity to Ejaz Pathan, the accused in the 1993 Bombay Blasts, all happened around 1980. Ali Budesh, with his dignified and peaceful demeanor, earned the nickname "Swami ji" in the underworld. In reality, he was a gangster wanted in India, and he faced an entry ban in Dubai due to his criminal background. Ali Budesh completed his education in Pune, where his mother was from. His association with the international gangsters began when he came to Mumbai. Since 2007, he had been working as an associate of Babloo Srivastav, who was incarcerated in Bareilly Jail. Ali Budesh's primary role in India, especially in Mumbai, was to settle land disputes and collect a fee for his services. Ali Budesh was not only connected to the underworld but also maintained ties with security agencies in various countries. Although Ali Budesh had the blessing of Dawood Ibrahim, their relationship soured for some reason, leading Ali Budesh to work against Dawood Ibrahim. He began sharing information about D Company's operatives with security agencies worldwide.

Ali Budesh in his early years.

Ali Budesh in his early years.

Now we come to the real narrative.

Ali Budesh arrives at the Hind Jewellery shop in his Toyota car and enters the showroom. Two Afghan men catch his attention in the showroom and he tries to recognize them, but he can't. He proceeds towards the cash counter, where his cashier is seated.

Ali Budesh: Are these people here to buy something, Zain?

Cashier: No, these people have come to meet you.

Ali Budesh: Did they say anything about the work?

Cashier: No.

Ali Budesh: Send them to the office. Zain.

- Ali Budesh always utters the word "Zain" after completing his sentences. In Arabic, the word "Zain" means beautiful.

Ali Budesh enters his cabin-like office, and after he leaves, the cashier speaks to the Afghan men:

Cashier: You guys can go to the office right in front. Swami ji can meet you there.

Afghani : Thank you, sir. By God, the goods here in Swami ji's shop are of excellent quality.

While talking, both Afghan men head to Ali Budesh's office.

Afghani : Assalamu Alaikum, Ali bhai.

Ali Budesh: Wa Alaikum Assalam Miyan, come inside and have a seat, please. Zain.

Both Afghan men sit on the chairs placed in the office and look around.

Ali Budesh: What will you have?

Afghani : Huzoor, we are ready to complete the task assigned to us.

Ali Budesh: Task? Whose task?

Afghani : Huzoor, you had requested a meeting with Brother Sami ul Haq, you had extended an invitation for him to come to Bahrain. We are merely carrying out Brother Sami's instructions.

Upon hearing this, a spark of excitement lights up Ali Budesh's eyes, and he enthusiastically remarks:

Ali Budesh: Seeing you was a pleasure, and you arrived so promptly.

Afghani : "Ali Bhai, I thought we should meet and move the relationship forward, and..........."

Ali Budesh: "The relationship has grown, my friends. Now, please introduce yourselves."

Afghani: "Abu Zar and Abid."

Ali Budesh: "Tonight, we have a party for you. Abu Zar bhai, did Sami ul Haq come as well?"

Abu Zar: "Ali Bhai, you know how strict things are these days for coming and going. Sami ul Haq bhai will come and meet you soon. Just wait a few more days."

Ali Budesh: "Since you've just arrived, let's have some fun. Today, we'll show you a Pakistani mujra, and you'll experience our hospitality too, Zain."

Saying this, Ali Budesh picked up the intercom in front of him and dialed a number.

Ali Budesh: "Our guests have arrived from a distance. Bring tea, water, and some food."

After saying this, Ali Budesh placed the intercom back on the table

Gold Market - Manama City - Bahrain

and turned to the Afghani individual.

Ali Budesh: Tonight at exactly 9 o'clock, we will meet at Adhari Hotel. There's an outlet of my friend there, featuring Pakistani mujra performances. We'll watch the mujra and have conversations as well.

Abu Zar : Wallah, just as I heard about you, your hospitality is indeed admirable.

The door to Ali Budesh's cabin opens, and a man brings tea and some food.

Ali Budesh: If Sami ul Haq brother also joins, then the atmosphere will be even more festive.

After a long silence, Abid says.

Abid : Ali bhai, Sami ul Haq brother will come and the work will progress tremendously.

Ali Budesh Inshallah.

Abid: Inshallah, your meeting with Sami ul Haq brother will happen very soon.

Ali Budesh: Ameen. OHHH.... Abid bhai, Abu bhai, do have some tea.

Both Afghani men start sipping their tea.

Ali Budesh: And tell me, how was your journey to get here?

Abid: The journey was quite fine.

Abu Zar: It wasn't fine, Ali bhai? We were supposed to come directly from Turkey to you. But the plan changed at the last moment. We had to go to Kabul, and from Kabul to Baluchistan. After spending a few days in Baluchistan, now both of us are here in Manama City, Bahrain, in front of you.

Ali Budesh: Well, now you're here. By the way, was there anything special in Baluchistan?

Abid: Yes, Ali bhai, there was something special. You will hear about it soon, regarding the work.

Ali Budesh: Zain.

Abu Zar: Ali bhai, let's meet you in the hotel this evening.

Ali Budesh: Insha'Allah, I'll be waiting for you.

After that, Abid and Abu Zar bid farewell to Ali Budesh. Once Abid and Abu Zar leave, Ali Budesh takes out his mobile phone from his pocket and calls his friend Peter Paul David.

- Brief Introduction of Peter Paul David - Peter Paul David is a Pakistani citizen and a close friend of Ali Budesh. He operates a dance and bar outlet at Hotel Adhari (Bahrain). Additionally, Peter Paul David runs an outlet of dance bars in Bangkok as well. Both Peter Paul David and Ali Budesh were arrested in Bahrain after the 9/11 attacks in the United States. They were arrested as suspects and spent 6 months in Bahrain's jail. During their time in Bahrain's jail, their friendship grew stronger. Some people in Bahrain even say that Ali Budesh helped set up Peter Paul David's business.

Ali Budesh: Hello Peter Bhai.

Peter Paul David: Salaam Ali Bhai.

Ali Budesh: Salaam. Tonight, I and a few others will come to your outlet. We should have a good dance performance at your outlet tonight.

Peter Paul David: Your wish is my command, Ali Bhai.

Ali Budesh: Good day.

Peter Paul David: Bye.

After this, Ali Budesh attempts to make a WhatsApp call to a number in India but doesn't receive any response. This number belongs to a don who is imprisoned in an Indian jail. Following this, Ali Budesh makes another call, this time to a number in Dubai, which belongs to Imran.

Ali Budesh: Hello Imran Bhai.

Imran: Wa-Alaikum-Salaam Swami Ji, tell me how can I help you ??

Ali Budesh: Imran Bhai, I'm not able to connect with them in India. Maybe the dabba (box) switched off. Please ensure my message reaches them.

- The code name for a mobile is "Dabba" Gangsters and mafia dons who are in jail refer to a mobile as Dabba. Dabba means mobile phone. "Dabba On Off" means turning the mobile on or off.

Imran: Swami Ji, Bhaiya has turned off the Dabba. The strictness has increased nowadays, and there have been checks in the past few days. I couldn't talk either. Once the Dabba is turned on, he will be able to talk to you.

Ali Budesh: Zain and Imran Bhai, everyone is fine??

Imran: Everyone is fine.

Ali Budesh: Alright, Imran Bhai, we'll talk later. Have a good day.

Imran: Alright, Swami Ji.

At around 9 PM, Ali Budesh meets Peter Paul David enthusiastically at the Adhari Hotel. Peter Paul David takes Ali Budesh to his office-like cabin in the Mujra outlet.

Peter Paul David: Ali Bhai, please have a seat.

Ali Budesh: Thank you, Zain.

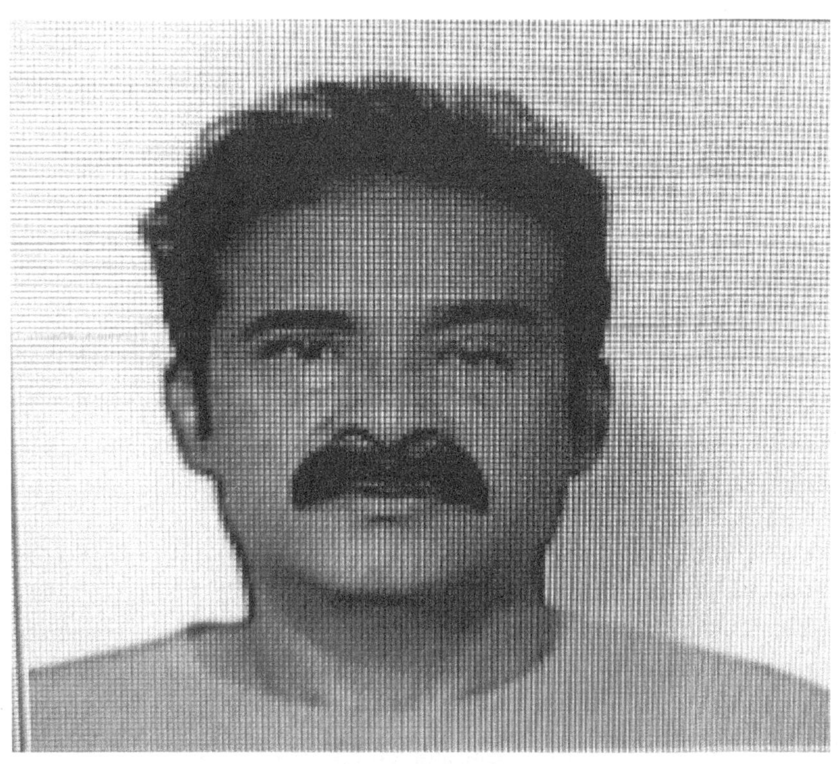

Peter Paul David

Peter Paul David: How may I assist you?

Ali Budesh: Your assistance will always be valued, but at this moment, some of my Afghan friends are coming to your Mujra bar. I need to meet and talk to them and I need your place.

Peter Paul David: Well, this outlet is yours, Ali Bhai. Just give the command.

Ali Budesh: Zain, it's your affection, Peter Bhai.

Peter Paul David: I'll arrange tea for you.

With these words, Peter Paul David steps out of his cabin and walks from the Mujra dance floor to the makeup room. The waiter serves Ali Budesh tea and Ali Budesh keeps an eye on the people coming and going through the glass doors of the cabin. He checks his watch, it's already 9:15, and the Afghanis haven't arrived yet. Where are these Afghanis? Before Ali Budesh can think further, he spots the two Afghanis entering the Afghan Mujra outlet.

Seeing both Afghanis, Ali Budesh steps out of his cabin, raising one hand to catch the attention of the two men. They both look at Ali Budesh and start walking towards him.

Ali Budesh: What's up, brothers? Running late, huh?

Abu Zar: Yes, Ali Bhai, got caught up in some work.

Ali Budesh: Even here, work? Take a break, you guys. Zain, have a bit of fun here; work is always there.

Abid: Ali Bhai is right.

Ali Budesh: Alright, let's show you the Mujra.

Ali Budesh leads both Afghanis to a private room where four girls are performing a Mujra dance on the floor. Ali Budesh and the Afghans take their seats in the available space. At the same time, a playlist of songs for a requested program is placed on their table.

Abid: Huzoor, my request is - bollywood hindi song "inhi logo ne le liya dupatta mera".

Abid's playful request brings laughter, and both Afghanis enjoy the Mujra dance with enthusiasm. As the icing on the cake, Ali Budesh hands them a wad of notes, and they start showering the money on the dancers without hesitation.

Abu Zar: Ali Bhai, this was so much fun.

Ali Budesh: Zain, Abu Bhai, let's go to my cabin now. We can discuss some work matters along with the party.

Abid: Wallah, sure thing.

Ali Budesh, Abu Zar, and Abid head to Peter Paul David's office-like cabin.

Ali Budesh: How's everything in Turkey?

Abid: All is well, but even while in Turkey, we have to be a bit cautious.

Ali Budesh: Khuda khair kare (May God keep you safe)

At that moment, Peter Paul David enters his cabin and switches on the TV, tuning in to a Pakistani news channel where a breaking news story is being reported.

News Anchor: "An attack has taken place on paramilitary forces in Quetta, resulting in casualties among the soldiers. TTP has claimed responsibility for this attack. With TTP at the helm, one wonders how long the people of Pakistan will continue to be targeted."

- TTP, which stands for Tehrik-e-Taliban Pakistan, is a terror group that has been declared as such by various nations, including the

United Nations, Pakistan, China, Canada, the United Kingdom, and the United States of America. TTP's primary goal is to carry out terrorist activities in Pakistan, including targeted killings, kidnappings, and bomb blasts, to generate funds. TTP's headquarters are located in eastern Afghanistan, and interestingly, the group operates its operations from Turkey. Besides this, their major objective is to expel Pakistani armed forces from FATA (Federally Administered Tribal Areas). TTP consists of approximately 5000 members and has been responsible for over 100 bomb blast incidents in Pakistan by 2018. The extent of their power can be gauged from the fact that they ran illicit telephone exchanges in Pakistan, facilitating money laundering and providing illegal instructions to their group members. In 2013, the Pakistani government shut down an illicit telephone exchange in Lahore. TTP's influence was such that they even kidnapped the son of former Prime Minister Yousuf Raza Gilani. There are speculations of a deal between TTP and Yousuf Raza Gilani's family, as his son Ali Haider Gilani returned three years later. TTP's involvement has even been alleged in the assassination of Benazir Bhutto.

As the Pakistani news anchor's background continues to play on the TV screen, Ali Budesh's attention isn't focused on the television but rather on Abid and Abu Zar. Upon seeing Abid and Abu Zar smiling while looking at Ali Budesh, a sense of camaraderie fills the room.

Ali Budesh: Am I understanding this correctly?

Abid: Sab khuda ki rehmat hai (It's all by the grace of God.)

Abed and Abu Zar were couriers for TTP, tasked with following the orders of their boss sami ul Haq while staying in Turkey. Their responsibilities included gathering information, attending meetings on sami ul Haq's behalf, and delivering messages. Upon sami ul Haq's instructions, Abu Zar and Abid traveled to Bahrain to meet Ali Budesh.

Ali Budesh: Does this mean that TTP wants the Pakistani Army to withdraw from the FATA area? Zain?

Without directly responding to Ali Budesh's question, Abid says:sami ul Haq had mentioned that you have some tasks for us. That's why we've come to Bahrain. Please issue your orders.

- sami ul haq was born on December 1, 1983, in Peshawar. He holds a Pakistani citizenship with the number 17301-1298455-3. He joined TTP soon after stepping into his youth. Despite being a Pakistani citizen, he resided in Turkey and operated a network for TTP, involving activities like kidnapping and targeted killings. In a short span of time, sami ul haq established a significant position within TTP.
- His Pakistani passport, which was renewed in 2020, carries the number AK - 5294555. He frequently traveled using this passport and held meetings in different countries. The main focus of these meetings was to recruit local and small-scale gang members into TTP. sami ul haq collaborated with local mafia and gangsters to facilitate targeted killings and kidnappings. He would distribute a percentage of the proceeds from these criminal activities among the gang members, along with funds for their monthly expenses.
- Any local gangsters or mafia members who refused to join forces with sami ul haq would face dire consequences orchestrated by other gang members, as sami ul haq had the power to eliminate those who opposed him. sami ul haq often organized meetings in third-party countries, and interestingly, he managed to avoid coming onto the radar of any security agency.
- In recent years, sami ul haq traveled to various countries, including the United Arab Emirates, Saudi Arabia, Africa, Nepal, and the United Kingdom, using his Pakistani passport. Notably,

his meeting in Bahrain with Ali Budesh was arranged by sending Abid and Abu Zar to meet Ali. sami ul haq wanted to gauge the benefits of meeting Ali Budesh in Bahrain before attending the meeting himself. Ali Budesh and TTP's friendship began in 2017. In 2017, Uzair Akbar arrived in Bahrain. He was from Balochistan and a collaborator of sami ul haq . Their professional acquaintance quickly evolved into a strong friendship after their initial meeting. Uzair Akbar was responsible for initiating contact between sami ul haq and Ali Budesh over a phone call in 2017, which marked the beginning of their ongoing communication.

Ali Budesh: Zain, the work is there, but I would prefer if you could arrange for me to discuss this matter with sami ul haq bhai. It would be better.

Abid: Tomorrow afternoon, we will come to you, and if it's Allah's will, we will facilitate a video conference for you to talk to sami ul haq bhai.

Ali Budesh: Insha'Allah.

Abid, Abu Zar, and Ali Budesh dine together at Peter Paul David's outlet. After dinner, Abid and Abu Zar bid farewell to Ali Budesh. Ali Budesh gets into his car, and just then, his mobile phone rings. He checks the screen and sees an incoming call from a US number. Though the number is new, he knows who it is.

Ali Budesh: Hello.

Arun: How are you, Swami Ji?

Ali Budesh: Zain Arun, bhai, all is well due to your blessings. Arun bhai I have been trying to call you for quite some time, but your call wasn't going through. Everything is fine ?

Arun: Swamiji, this is a prison, and here one has to take care of oneself. The conditions in this jail are quite strict, so even keeping this phone hidden requires caution. I just turned on this phone. I activated a new virtual number and called Imran in Dubai. He told me that you wanted to talk.

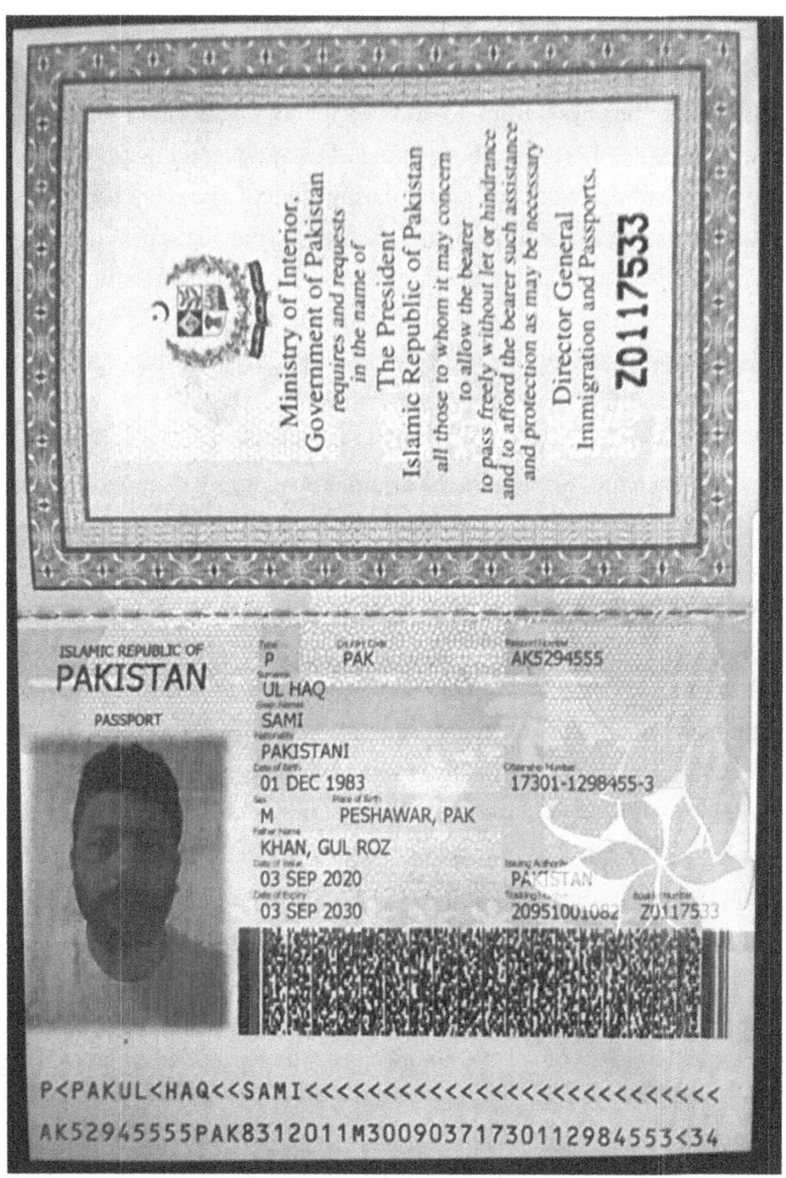

Ministry of Interior,
Government of Pakistan
requires and requests
in the name of
The President
Islamic Republic of Pakistan
all those to whom it may concern
to allow the bearer
to pass freely without let or hindrance
and to afford the bearer such assistance
and protection as may be necessary.
Director General
Immigration and Passports.
Z01117533

ISLAMIC REPUBLIC OF
PAKISTAN
PASSPORT

P PAK AK5294555
UL HAQ
SAMI
PAKISTANI
01 DEC 1983 17301-1298455-3
M PESHAWAR, PAK
KHAN, GUL ROZ
03 SEP 2020 PAKISTAN
03 SEP 2030 20951001082 Z01117533

P<PAKUL<HAQ<<SAMI<<<<<<<<<<<<<<<<<<<<<<<<<<<
AK52945555PAK8312011M30090371730112984553<34

Sami ul Haq Passport

- Arun Srivastava is a don who was arrested in Singapore in 1995 and extradited to India from there. He used to reside in Dubai and operated his mafia business from there. Despite being born in India, Arun Srivastava held Nepali citizenship and used a Nepali passport. He got involved in the world of crime during his college days in Lucknow. After entering the criminal world, he formed connections with a Nepali Cabinet Minister and mafia members. His association with Nepali gangsters and the Cabinet Minister ran so deep that the Cabinet Minister facilitated Arun Srivastava in obtaining Nepali citizenship. This enabled him to acquire a Nepali passport, which he used to travel worldwide.

  In India, Arun Srivastava had numerous criminal cases registered against him, but due to his Nepali citizenship, he was never apprehended. While red corner notices were issued based on the cases registered in India, he remained elusive by traveling using his Nepali passport. During his stay in Dubai, he interacted with individuals from the D Company and Chhota Rajan's group. In fact, Indian news channels had even begun referring to Arun Srivastava as an operative of the D Company. He had a keen interest in casinos and often traveled to countries like Hong Kong and Singapore to gamble. In 1995, while he was in Singapore to gamble, Interpol received a tip-off that Arun Srivastava, traveling on a Nepali passport, was one of India's most wanted criminals. As soon as he landed in Singapore, he was arrested and the Indian Embassy was informed. Despite his claims of Nepali citizenship, the Indian Embassy confirmed that Arun Srivastava was Indian, not Nepali. While his case was forwarded to Nepal, India presented solid evidence to prove his Indian identity, categorizing him as a wanted criminal. Arun Srivastava had used his Indian passport to travel Singapore in 1991, The entry for that passport was recorded in Singapore, indicating that in the travel history of the Indian passport from 1991, the Singaporean government recognized Arun Srivastava as an Indian citizen and affirmed India's claim. It is also said that a substantial amount, including ₹20 lakhs, was spent on this, with D

Company providing the funds. Arun Srivastava faced legal proceedings in India and was sentenced to imprisonment. This individual is none other than Babloo Srivastava, who is currently incarcerated in Bareilly Central Jail.

Ali Budesh: Arun Bhai, the carrier pigeons from Adnan have arrived with a letter.

- Adnan is the code name for sami ul haq . In phone conversations among the mafia and criminals, real names are not used. This practice is to ensure that if someone is eavesdropping on their calls, they won't be able to identify the individuals involved. Therefore, Ali Budesh has been given the code name "Swami Ji," and sami ul haq has been given the code name "Adnan."

Arun: If Adnan is ready to proceed with this work, we can secure $10 million from Washington.

Ali Budesh: InshaAllah.

Arun: Swami Ji, just keep following my instructions. You just need to act accordingly. The $10 million is just an excuse; in reality, we need to do something good for this country. Even though I'm in jail, my country is still India. We need to eliminate the traitors within the country. While some people show their patriotism on Twitter and Facebook, I want to take action against the enemies of the nation. Tomorrow, when Adnan's pigeons arrive, give an advance of 50,000 hare (green) to them . Remember, we need Adnan's network. I've spent years planning this mission, and I've already collected some funds from patriotic individuals for this purpose. The funds are with Imran in Dubai. You and Imran will contribute funds to Adnan's network. I'll tell Imran to reach Bahrain to meet you..

- "Hare" means dollars. In the criminal world, currencies also have code names. The term "hare" is used for dollars because the color of dollars is green. Due to this green color, the code name for dollars became "hare." Similarly, the British pounds are referred to as “shine” due to their color, and Dubai’s dirham is called “glow.”

Ali Budesh: Arun bhai, I will do as you say. Zain and Insha’Allah, you will succeed.

Arun: What message do Adnan’s pigeons bring?

Ali Budesh: Arun bhai, tomorrow there will be a video conference.

Arun: Swami ji, during the video conference, you will only talk about giving the money to sami ul haq for our work. Tell them that sami ul haq will get a good amount of money. However, in return for this, sami ul haq will have to do some tasks for us. If necessary, sami ul haq will be informed about what we need and when. For now, just tell Adnan to ensure the stability of his network in Lahore and to complete the training of the fidayeen. Besides that, we will need RDX.

Ali Budesh: Arun bhai, alright, I’ll say the same thing tomorrow. By the way, Arun bhai, what’s going on in your mind?

Arun: Hahaha, Swami ji, you’ll find out soon. Just keep doing what I’m telling you to do. You’ve been connected with me for so many years, just keep being my front. Do as much as I say.

Ali Budesh: Absolutely, Arun bhai, I always do what you ask me to do. I’ll provide you with the report of tomorrow’s meeting.

Arun: If my dabba gets off, leave the details with Imran in Dubai for me. As soon as the opportunity arises, I’ll get in touch with Imran. Okay, bye.

Ali Budesh: Good night.

Ali Budesh puts his phone back in his pocket and starts his car’s ignition, heading towards his home. Peter Paul David stands near the hotel’s exit, observing Ali Budesh as he departs.

The next day, in the afternoon, Abid and Abu Zarr arrive at Hind Jewelers with a briefcase in hand. Ali Budesh is already present at the showroom, browsing through some jewelry pieces at the counter. Abid and Abu Zarr enter the showroom, offering greetings to Ali Budesh. Ali Budesh escorts them to his office-like cabin.

Ali Budesh: "The night must have been peaceful."

Abid: "Indeed, I had a restful sleep."

Ali Budesh: "When are you planning to have a conversation with Sami ul Haq?"

By ignoring Ali Budesh words, Abu Zarr takes a high-security laptop and a satellite phone from the briefcase. He turns on both devices and opens his laptop. A password window appears on the laptop screen, and he positions the laptop in front of Abid. Abid uses a device to input the password, and through the satellite phone, establishes a connection with an IP address in North Korea.

Abid: "Just 2 minutes."

Ali Budesh: "Zain."

Abid opens a software on the laptop. This software is designed for secure video calls. Such software is used either by security agencies or by groups that pay a hefty price for it. The software establishes a video call connection, and the screen displays the face of Sami ul Haq. As soon as his face appears, Abid and Abu Zarr simultaneously greet him, saying, "Salam Alekum Bhai Jaan."

Sami ul Haq: "Waalekum Salam."

Abid: "Bhai, have you spoken to Swami Ji on the phone yet? Now you can meet face-to-face."

As Abid says this, he pushes the laptop towards Ali Budesh.

Ali Budesh: "Salam Sami Bhai."

Sami ul Haq: "Waalekum Salam, Swami Ji. Until now, I had only heard your voice. Today, I've had the pleasure of seeing you as well. You're shining like the moon. Hahaha."

- Ali Budesh had a completely bald head, and due to the lack of hair, his head appeared shiny. In a playful manner, Sami ul Haq compared Ali Budesh's head to the moon.

Ali Budesh: "Well, the moon is right on my head, Sami Bhai, and today you've had the chance to witness this moon too."

Sami ul Haq: "Swami Ji, it seems you took offense. Anyway, please tell me what task you have for me?"

Ali Budesh: "There's a substantial amount of work, and we'll make every effort to pay a price worthy of it, Insha'Allah. But you have some special tasks to perform for us."

Sami ul Haq: "How so?"

Ali Budesh: "You'll be informed about the details when the time comes. For now, you need to focus on getting your network strong in Lahore. Additionally, keep a tight hold on resources like RDX."

"We'll also need some mujahideen."

Sami ul Haq: "What's the plan, brother?"

Ali Budesh: "The plan will be shared with you at the right time. As a gesture of goodwill, I will provide Abid with $50,000 today, and you'll continue to receive funds as needed. Use this money for your operations."

Sami ul Haq: "Swami Ji, whenever you need anything, Insha'Allah, I will provide it for you."

Ali Budesh: "Zain, for today, that's all. We'll stay in touch."

Sami ul Haq: "Swami Ji, Abid will give you a new number that will only work on WhatsApp and Telegram. If you need to talk about something, you can contact me through that number."

Ali Budesh: "Alright, have a good day."

Sami ul haq : Khuda Hafiz.

As soon as sami ul haq says "Khuda Hafiz," his video disappears from the laptop screen. Ali Budesh takes out a bag from his table and gives $50,000 to Abid. Abid takes the $50000 and puts it in his pocket. After securing the money, Abid and Abu Zar bid farewell to Ali Budesh and leave the showroom.

After Abid and Abu Zar leave, Ali Budesh receives a WhatsApp call on his phone, and the caller's number is from Israel. Ali Budesh answers the call, and the caller is Imran.

Ali Budesh: Hello.

Imran: Swami Ji's I got a message from bhaiya; he was saying that I should meet you.

Ali Budesh: Zain, come over whenever you can.

Imran: I'll be there by the day after tomorrow.

Ali Budesh: Ok come over & Have a good day.

- Imran's real name is Sanjay Tiwari. Sanjay Tiwari is also a resident of Lucknow (Uttar Pradesh) and has been involved in some criminal activities, leading to his incarceration. It was during his time in jail that he crossed paths with Arun Srivastava, and this encounter transformed not only into a friendship but also into a business relationship between the two. After being released from jail, he began working for Arun Srivastava.
- Imran, or Sanjay Tiwari, had a specific role. He would collect

information about his targets, interact with people involved in cases, and the money given for these tasks was handed over to Imran. Another significant aspect of Imran's role was that he would meticulously maintain surveillance on his assigned targets. In Arun Srivastava's plans, both Ali Budesh and Sanjay Tiwari played crucial roles. Ali Budesh would operate in the front, following Arun's instructions, while Sanjay Tiwari, or Imran, would stay near the target, collecting all the necessary information and passing it on to Arun Srivastava.

- Whenever Sanjay Tiwari met anyone, he introduced himself as Imran. He chose the name Imran as a cover for his missions. For this mission, he adopted the name Imran, and in Islamic countries where he operated, people assumed he was a Muslim due to his name. This perception allowed him to gather information from people who shared information with him, believing he was a fellow Muslim.

Ali Budesh places his mobile phone on one side and picks it up again after a few seconds. He calls Arun in India. Ali Budesh dials the same number from which he received the call. The call connects, and Arun speaks from the other side.

Arun: Yes, Swami Ji, please tell me.

Ali Budesh: Arun Bhai, I spoke to Adnan. We had a video call, and I conveyed exactly what you had instructed. Additionally, I've given Adnan's messenger 50,000 in cash, as you had mentioned.

Arun: Alright, Swami Ji. Please wait for my next instructions. I've messaged Imran, and he will be arriving from Dubai soon. I'm closing the box now; we'll discuss the rest later.

Ali Budesh: Good day.

Ali Budesh takes his mobile phone and steps out of his cabin to attend to the customers in the showroom. No customer at the Hind Jeweler store could have imagined that the owner of Hind Jewelry, Ali Budesh, is a wanted gangster.

In life, most people live with two faces and present different personas. Ali Budesh was living a similar life. He was a prominent gold businessman in Bahrain but also a wanted criminal in the rest of the world.

At 10 PM, while Ali Budesh is leaving his jewelry showroom, he receives a WhatsApp call on his mobile phone from sami ul haq . Ali Budesh answers the call.

Ali Budesh: Hello.

Sami ul haq : Swami Ji, in 2 days, one of my associates will meet you. He will provide full support for your mission. Whatever you need, you can tell him whatever you need in Lahore. He is on his way to meet you and His name is Eid Gul.

Ali Budesh: Okay, thank you, Zain.

Sami ul haq : Khuda Hafiz.

Ali Budesh: Good night.

- Eid Gul: In reality, Eid Gul was the younger brother of sami ul haq . He was born on January 1, 1987, in Pakistan. Eid Gul served as a handler for sami ul haq's network, especially in Lahore and the Baloch area. He was responsible for recruiting new boys for the TTP (Tehrik-i-Taliban Pakistan) and sending those boys to Turkey for jihadist training under Sami ul Haq . Eid Gul also managed the supply network for explosives. He facilitated the distribution of RDX for blasts across Pakistan as per the requirements. He was an explosives expert himself and provided blast training to newly recruited boys in the TTP. Recently, he carried out suicide bombings in Pakistan, preparing and deploying human bombers.

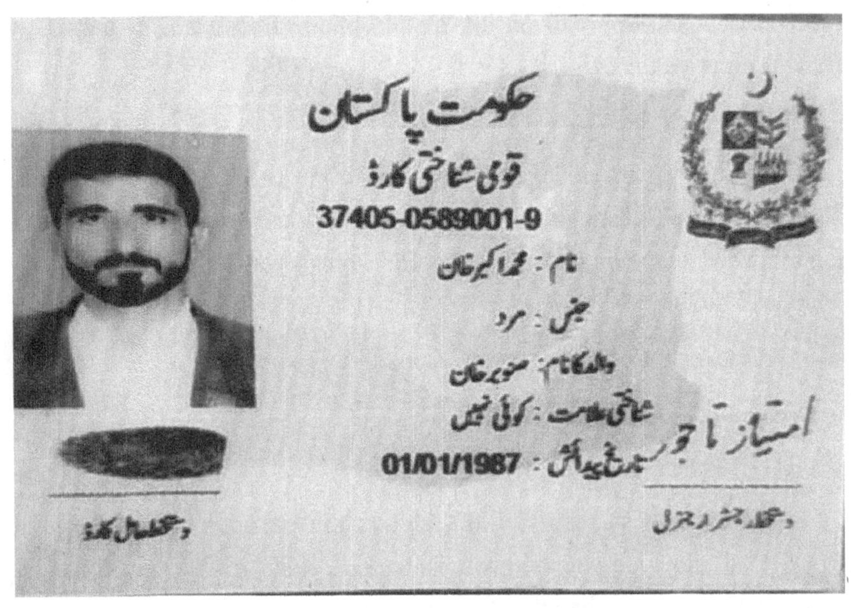

حکومت پاکستان

قومی شناختی کارڈ

37405-0589001-9

نام : محمد اکبر خان

جنس : مرد

والد کا نام : صنوبر خان

شناختی علامت : کوئی نہیں

تاریخ پیدائش : 01/01/1987

امتیاز تاجور

دستخط حامل کارڈ

دستخط رجسٹرار جنرل

Eid Gul

The next morning at 11:30 AM, Imran takes a flight from Dubai to Bahrain and lands in the capital city of Manama. After landing, Imran calls Ali Budesh from outside the airport.

Ali Budesh: Hello.

Imran: Swami ji, I'm in your city.

Ali Budesh: Welcome, Imran bhai. Weren't you supposed to come tomorrow?

Imran: Swami ji, I didn't have any important work in Dubai, so I thought I'd leave early.

Ali Budesh: Zain, you did well. I have arranged your stay. The arrangement is at the same place as before, and the meeting will be at the Peter Paul David outlet for the party tonight.

Imran: Who is Peter Paul David, Swami ji?

Ali Budesh: He's a friend and an associate for our work.

Imran: Hmm, alright Swami ji, I'll see you in the evening then.

Ali Budesh: 9 PM, Hotel Adhari, Mujra Outlet.

Imran: Mujra? That's quite common even in Dubai. Alright, let's meet in the evening at 9.

Ali Budesh: Good day.

At exactly 9 PM, Imran arrives at Hotel Adhari and waits outside. He impatiently smokes a cigarette, repeatedly taps his wristwatch, and scans the crowd for Ali Budesh. As he waits, a car pulls up in front of him, and Ali Budesh steps out.

Imran: is on edge, his cigarette in hand, and he watches Ali Budesh as he emerges from the car.

Imran: Swami ji, you arrives late I hope everything is fine with you ?

Ali Budesh: Imran bhai, I'm sorry, I had to go to the hospital for a check-up. It took some time there. Let's go inside.

Ali Budesh and Imran enter Hotel Adhari's mujra bar. Imran enjoys the beauty of the place as they enter. Both of them don't say anything to anyone and take their respective seats at an empty table.

Imran: Swami ji, are you doing well? Was there a need to go to the hospital?

Ali Budesh: It was a routine check-up at the Army Hospital. But in reality, there was quite a bit of swelling in my legs due to high sugar levels. So, I had to go there.

Imran: Are you fine now? Ali Budesh By Allah's grace, I'm fine, Zain. But tell me, how was your journey?

Imran: The journey was fine. It wasn't a long flight, just 1 hour and 20 minutes. After arriving, I went straight to the guest house and fell asleep. As soon as I woke up, I came straight to you.

Ali Budesh: Zain, after coming here, did you talk to Arun bhai?

Imran: No, Swami ji, but I messaged him. You know how constrained he is and how he manages even while being inside. Security checks are ongoing in jail, and phones are not allowed. But Arun bhai is managing somehow. He doesn't spare the enemies of the country, whether it's Nepal's Dilshad Mirza Beg, Yunus Ansari, or Jamim Shah. By eliminating them all, bhaiya destroyed the entire network of Indian fake currency. Now, the influx of Indian fake currency from Nepal has stopped.

Ali Budesh: Zain, Arun bhai's planning is foolproof. No one can predict what his next move will be. We have no idea about the mission he's on this time, not even a hint.

Ali Budesh

Ali Budesh Outside his Shop

Interrupting Ali Budesh, Imran says:

Imran: Swami ji, my work is just as much as bhaiya tells me, not more than that. We don't need to know the target of the mission; bhaiya's command is sufficient for us.

Ali Budesh: Zain, may Allah grant Arun bhai a long life. It's Arun bhai's determination alone that even while inside the jail, he's eliminating India's enemies.

Finishing his sentence, Ali Budesh signals a waiter to come over.

Waiter: Yes, sir.Ali Budesh: Hasn't Peter Bhai arrived?

Waiter: Peter sir is busy in a staff meeting.

Ali Budesh: Alright, when he's free, tell him that I'm remembering him..

Ali Budesh gives the waiter an order for dinner. The waiter takes the order and leaves. Just then, a dance performance featuring two girls starts on the stage. Ali Budesh and Imran begin watching the dance. Just at that moment, Peter Paul David arrives at the venue.

Ali Budesh: Please, Peter bhai, have a seat with us.

Peter Paul David takes a seat next to Ali Budesh and says as he sits:

Peter Paul David: Salaam aleikum, Ali bhai.

Ali Budesh: Wa aleikum assalam. Meet Imran, our friend who has come from Dubai.

Peter Paul David: Salaam, Imran bhai.

Imran: Wa alaikum salaam.

Peter Paul David: Imran bhai, are you from Dubai?

Before Imran can respond, Ali Budesh answers:

Ali Budesh: Peter bhai, Imran bhai is originally from India and settled in Dubai.

Peter Paul David: Good.

Ali Budesh: Imran, Peter Paul David is from Pakistan and he's a flamboyant king of the dance bars and nightclubs in Bahrain and Thailand. He's a dear friend of ours and quite skilled in his work.

Imran: Khushamdeed, Peter bhai. Where in Pakistan are you from?

Peter Paul David: I'm from Karachi. But I don't travel to Karachi much these days. Business is here, and even my family has settled here. We only go to Karachi with the family during holidays, occasionally.

Imran: Alright.

After this, Ali Budesh, Imran, and Peter Paul David sit together for dinner. During the course of the meeting, Ali Budesh invites Imran to visit his gold showroom the next day. Imran confirms a time of 2 PM the next afternoon. After finishing dinner, the three bid farewell to each other. Ali Budesh leaves in his car for his home, while Imran takes a taxi to his guest house.

- This was Imran's first meeting with Peter Paul David. As long as Imran stayed in Bahrain, he would frequently join Ali Budesh for dinner at the bar and mujra outlet owned by Peter Paul David.

The next day, around 2 PM, Imran arrives at Hind Jewelers, and Ali Budesh guides him to his office cabin. Imran takes a seat and starts smoking a cigarette after taking a pack out of his pocket. Meanwhile, Ali Budesh speaks to his cashier through the intercom.

Ali Budesh: Send some tea and snacks.

Cashier: Yes, I'll send them right away.

Ali Budesh places the intercom receiver on the table and, while Imran continues to smoke, he says:

Ali Budesh: Imran bhai, I'm still wondering what Arun bhai is planning this time. Has he given any hint yet?

Imran: Swami ji, what will you do with hints? Bhaiya is deeply engrossed in patriotic fervor. His planning will likely revolve around capturing someone from the list of most wanted criminals.

Ali Budesh: Zain, I'm thinking..........

Before this, Ali Budesh finishes his conversation. Ali Budesh's mobile phone rings. The caller ID shows the number flashing as Arvind Ojha - AAJ TAK. Ali Budesh looks at the flashing number on the phone for a moment and then speaks slowly, "Why am I receiving a call from Aaj Tak?" With a hesitant tone, Ali Budesh answers the call.

Ali Budesh: Hello.

Arvind Ojha: Ali Budesh, this is Arvind Ojha from Aaj Tak. Ali Bhai, I have some questions to ask you.

Ali Budesh: Regarding what matters?

Arvind Ojha: Ali Bhai, some calls and messages are being sent from your side to BJP leaders, warning them to pay 10 lakh or face dire consequences.

Ali Budesh: No, I have nothing to do with such things here. If you ask me, I will tell you the truth.

Arvind Ojha: So, someone is plotting against you?

Ali Budesh: Yes, Chhota Shakeel is behind this conspiracy. I have never been involved in extortion, Arvind Bhai.

Arvind Ojha: Why do you think Chhota Shakeel is using your name for extortion?

Ali Budesh: Look, chhota shakeel is nobody now he has no power left chhota shakeel is nobody chhota shakeel is nothing. That's why he's using my name for extortion to make some money in my name.

Arvind Ojha: I see.

Ali Budesh: I'll say it again, I have no involvement in extortion. All of this is Chhota Shakeel's conspiracy.

Arvind Ojha: Okay.

Ali Budesh: Alright, good day.

As soon as Ali Budesh disconnected his mobile phone after saying this much, Imran was observing and listening carefully. As soon as Ali Budesh disconnected the call, Imran spoke.

Imran: Swami Ji, the D Company seems to be quite interested in you. D Company sending extortion messages in your name to BJP leaders?

Before Imran could finish his sentence, Ali Budesh interjected.

Ali Budesh: Forget about all of this. Imran bhai, the TV channels will now get high TRP ratings in my name. The interviews from Aaj Tak will be running day and night, and the D Company folks will keep cursing me.

Imran: Hahaha, and Swami Ji Bhaiya really shattered Pakistan's backbone. Pakistan used to send counterfeit currency from Nepal to India, and Bhaiya annihilated that whole network.

Ali Budesh: Zain, Arun bhai mentioned to me that he can get 10 million dollars from the American government. It's a substantial amount in my opinion. This time, Arun bhai seems to be targeting a most wanted individual from either America or India. That wanted person might be wanted by both India and America. But Arun bhai hasn't given any such hints. It's just a speculative thought.

Imran: Swami Ji, whatever bhaiya does, he does it with careful consideration.

At that moment, Imran's mobile receives a call from Arun. Imran puts his phone on speaker and answers the call.

Imran: Hello, bhaiya.

Arun: Hello. Is Swami Ji with you?

Imran: Yes, yes.

Arun: Okay, please pass the call to Swami Ji.

Imran: sir, the hands-free is on.

Ali Budesh: Arun bhai.

Arun: swami ji what's the news?

Ali Budesh: Arun bhai, Adnan called. A guy named Eid Gul is coming to meet me.

Arun: Oh, where is he coming from?

Ali Budesh: Adnan didn't mention that. He just said he's coming to meet and if I need anything I should inform Eid Gul needs anything.

Arun: Alright, things should go as planned. Adnan has gained confidence due to the 50,000 dollars he received. Otherwise, he wouldn't have sent someone so quickly. If you get any other details, let me know, and keep in touch with Imran.

Arun addresses Imran while on hands-free.

Arun: Imran, you should also meet Eid Gul and stay in touch with him. Listen carefully to everything he says and understand how much work Eid Gul can bring. I'm preparing the groundwork here, and it's serious. I'll call you tomorrow morning at 11.

Ali Budesh and Imran both say okay, bhaiya, and the call ends. They sit together in the office, drinking tea, and there is complete silence in the cabin. This silence is interrupted by the ringing of Ali Budesh's mobile phone. His phone number doesn't display on the screen; instead, it shows a private number. The screen of Ali Budesh's phone shows this to Imran, who also sees the private number displayed and tells Ali Budesh to answer it.

Ali Budesh puts his phone on speaker and answers the call.

Ali Budesh: Hello?

From the other side, it wasn't anyone else but Eid Gul, and he was using a secure burner phone that is difficult to trace.

Eid Gul: Swami ji?

Ali Budesh: Who are you?

Eid Gul: Swami ji, I am Eid Gul. sami ul haq 's brother, speaking. I am currently in Bahrain. Tell me when we can meet?

Ali Budesh: Zain, you're welcome to Bahrain. Let's meet this evening at 9 o'clock at Hotel Adhari.There My friend has a mujra and bar outlet we will meet there.

Eid Gul: I'll be there at 9 o'clock.

After saying this, Eid Gul hangs up the phone. After the call ends, Imran addresses Ali Budesh.

Imran: Swami ji, bhaiya was right in saying that they're rushing things due to the $50,000. They need more money, otherwise they wouldn't be in such a hurry. The TTP doesn't send anyone so quickly.

Ali Budesh: Your words are absolutely correct. Imran bhai, now we will see how skillful he is. So, let's meet at 9 o'clock in the evening. Now

I'll attend to a customer for a while.

Imran: Absolutely, Swami ji.

After saying that, Imran tucks the remaining cigarette into an ashtray on his table and bids farewell to Ali Budesh, heading to his guest house. Ali Budesh returns to attend to customers in his showroom.

Later that night, precisely at 9 o'clock, Ali Budesh arrives at the main gate of Hotel Adhari. He sees Imran already there, smoking a cigarette. Ali Budesh gets out of his car and approaches Imran. They exchange greetings and step inside together.

Ali Budesh: Good evening, Imran Bhai.

Imran: Good evening, Swami Ji.

Ali Budesh: Imran Bhai, did you arrive early? Zain?

Imran: No, Swami Ji, I just arrived. I came and lit a cigarette.

Ali Budesh: Zain, it seems like we'll have to wait for Eid Gul. How will we recognize Eid Gul? We've never seen him before.

Imran: Swami Ji, we don't need to recognize him. He will recognize us. You and I just need to do what Bhaiya tells us to do.

With this conversation, Imran started puffing his cigarette, and Ali Budesh stood by the gate, observing the people coming into the hotel from a distance. After a while, a taxi arrived and stopped there. From that taxi emerged a person with a clean-shaven, egg-shaped face, army-style haircut, and a small beard and mustache that resembled a Bollywood hero's style. This individual stepped out of the taxi and walked towards Ali Budesh, extending his right hand forward as he spoke.

Eid Gul: Swami Ji.

Ali Budesh: Yes?

Eid Gul: You don't recognize me? I am Eid Gul.

Ali Budesh held Eid Gul's extended hand in his own hand and, with joy, he said,

Ali Budesh: Zain, I had been waiting for you. Let's go inside, shall we? And let me introduce you to Imran. He works with me and resides in Dubai.

Eid Gul: Aasalamalekun, Imran bhai. So, you're from Dubai?

Imran: Wa Alaikum Assalam. Yes, I'm based in Dubai.

Ali Budesh: Formal introductions can wait. First, let's head inside the hotel. We can sit there comfortably and have a chat.

Imran and Eid Gul, accompanied by Ali Budesh, arrive at the Peter Paul David's dance and bar outlet within Hotel Adhari. They proceed towards a private hall, casting casual glances at the dancing ladies on the floor. Finding a suitable table, they sit down. Ali Budesh instructs Imran and Eid Gul to place their drink orders with the waiter. Eid Gul orders a refreshing drink, Imran opts for a Black and White Scotch, while Ali Budesh requests a well-cooked lamb dish. He also asks the waiter to bring Peter Paul David to their table.

Ali Budesh: Imran bhai, smoking so many cigarettes isn't good for your health.

Imran: Swami ji, I've developed a habit now. I don't even realize anything until I've finished three packs. My Lungs now used to it, if I don't smoke my lungs ask for smoke.

Ali Budesh: Being a chain smoker isn't right.

Imran: Swami ji, your sage advice is enlightening, hahaha.

Imran leaves his statement unfinished and gazes at Eid Gul with a calm demeanor, offering his attention.

Imran: Eid Gul bhai, where have you come from just now? I mean in Bahrain.

Eid Gul: From Dubai.

Imran: Dubai, what a coincidence! I also live in Dubai.

Eid Gul: Dubai is the right place to live. It offers peace.

Imran: You're absolutely right.

Before imran says anything more, Ali Budesh start talking to Eid Gul
Ali Budesh: Eid Gul bhai, we'll definitely need you. And you should stay in touch with Imran bhai because my health isn't stable. If I ever end up in the hospital, I have to stay there for 5 - 6 days. I have problems with high sugar and high blood pressure. sami ul haq bhai sent you here at the right time. Your meeting with Imran bhai has already happened, and he will handle everything.

Eid Gul: Alright, sir. By the way, could you please tell us what the matter is?

Now Imran Answer Eid Gul Query.

Imran: As told to Sami ul Haq, you need to reinforce your network in Lahore. We'll need explosives and weapons alongside the suicide bombers.

Eid Gul: Everything is being arranged in Lahore. I'll stay in Dubai for 2 days from Bahrain and then head to Lahore. We're setting up a new operation camp in Lahore. InshaAllah, our network will be up and running by next week. Just let me know what you need.

At that moment, Peter Paul David arrives and takes a seat next to Imran. Ali Budesh introduces Peter Paul David to Eid Gul.

Ali Budesh: Eid Gul, allow me to introduce Peter Paul David. He owns the bar and mujra outlet in this hotel. And Peter is from Karachi as well.he has a good Business Zain.

Eid Gul: Salam, Peter Bhai.

Peter Paul David: Waalekum Salam. Where are you from, brother?

Eid Gul: I'm also from Pakistan, but these days I'm back and forth between Dubai. Let's just say I'm currently in Dubai.

Peter Paul David: If it's meant to be, we might cross paths in Dubai too. I'm starting a business there as well—importing luxury cars. Import old cars from the US to Dubai and then export them to Pakistan. Eid Gul: Wallah, we definitely need those cars in Dubai and Pakistan as well. Your business is going to do well, Peter Bhai.

Peter Paul David: Certainly, whatever you need, just let me know. You'll get it.

Eid Gul: Absolutely.

In the midst of the conversation, Imran interjects.

Imran: Hey guys, are you going to handle all the business dealings today itself? We're here at Peter Bhai's place, let's enjoy some mujra along with the food.

Ali Budesh: When two people meet, business discussions are bound to happen, Zain.

Imran: Eid Gul bhai, if you need anything, just inform me, and also pass this message to Sami ul Haq. Let him know that I am the one point contact. By the way, I also reside in Dubai and this is my number. You can reach me at this number. Soon, I will inform you about work opportunities for you.

Eid Gul takes Imran's card and saves the mobile number provided on the card into his phone. He writes his own mobile number on the back of the same card and hands it over to Imran. Imran also adds his number to his mobile contact list. Eid Gul addresses Peter next.

Eid Gul: "Peter bhai, you should also provide your number. We can establish a business relationship." Peter Paul David: "Of course, I'll give you my business card. It has my mobile number, as well as the numbers for offices here and in Bangkok."

Eid Gul: "Your business is in Bangkok too?" Peter Paul David: "Yes, I also have bars and restaurants in Bangkok as part of my business."

Eid Gul: "Sounds impressive."

Peter Paul David takes out his business card and hands it to Eid Gul. Eid Gul saves all the numbers printed on the business card into his mobile phone. Meanwhile, Ali Budesh interjects: "Hey, if the number exchange is done, let's grab some food and drinks!"

All the people start eating quietly and nobody talks while eating. Just then, a waiter approaches the table and whispers something in Peter Paul David's ear. Peter Paul David bids farewell to Ali Budesh, Imran, and Eid Gul, then gets up from the table and heads towards his office. After Peter Paul David leaves, Eid Gul speaks to Imran:

Eid Gul: "Sami Ul haq bhai's call will come at 10:30 PM tonight. He mentioned that he'll call me after my meeting with Swami JI. Now Imran bhai you are also here you can too talk to him as you are one point contact .when the call comes, you can introduce yourself to Sami ul bhai too."

Imran: "Absolutely."

Ali Budesh: "You've got it right, Eid Gul bhai."

Ali Budesh looked at his wrist watch and says "It's 15 minutes until 10:30. In these 15 minutes, you all can enjoy eating, drinking, and the mujara."

Imran responds: “Swami Ji, all of this will continue happening.”

After saying this, Imran turns to Eid Gul and asks:

Imran:What kind of activities are you involved in, Gul Bhai??

Eid Gul: “I’m an explosives expert and Smi ul Haq’s younger brother. I handle the network for him.”

Imran: “Being an explosives expert, what all do you do?”

Eid Gul: “I work with time bombs, car bombs, detonators for road blasts, and much more.”

Imran: “That is great. Let’s raise a toast to this!”

Imran raises his scotch glass and says “Cheers,” while Eid Gul lifts his juice glass. They each take a sip from their glasses and begin to watch the mujara in peace. Right at 10:30, Eid Gul’s phone rings.

Eid Gul: “Hello, Sami ul Haq bhai”

Sami ul Haq: “Hello, what’s the news?”

Eid Gul: “I’m with Imran right now, and Swami Ji has introduced Imran as the one Point contact. Whatever needs to be discussed or arranged, Imran will handle.”

Sami ul Haq: “Alright. Since all are together, we can talk hands-free and discuss everything at once.”

Eid Gul switches his phone to speaker mode and places it between Ali Budesh and Imran. Both Imran and Ali Budesh greet Sami ul Haq simultaneously.

Sami ul Haq: “Hello, Salam. Swami Ji, are you heading somewhere? Is that why Imran is the one Point contact?”

Ali Budesh: "I'm not going anywhere. I've been feeling a bit unwell these days. That's why Imran is the right person. He handles everything for us, even our finances. He manages everything from Dubai."

Sami ul Haq: "Alright. Salam Alaikum, Imran bhai."

Imran: "Wa Alaikum Salam."

Sami ul Haq: "Imran bhai, you reside in Dubai. If we had spoken earlier, we could have met in Dubai. I used to live in Dubai too, but I had to leave Dubai and settle in Turkey. Anyway, Eid Gul will give my number to you, and we'll stay in direct touch."

Imran: "Absolutely. Now that we've met, whenever I visit Turkey, I'll definitely meet you. Otherwise, I'll stay in touch with you through calls once I'm in Dubai."

Sami ul Haq: "Sounds good, Imran bhai. Eid Gul, you should return to Dubai and then head to Lahore."

Eid Gul: "Sure, brother."

Sami ul Haq: "Khua Hafiz."

All three say "Khuda Hafiz" (God be with you) together, and Sami ul Haq disconnects the call.

Eid Gul: "Swami ji, thank you for the hospitality."

Ali Budesh: "A guest is like God, Zain. So, don't thank us."

Eid Gul: "Swami ji, I need some funds in advance. Apart from the 50,000 you gave us. I need additional advance."

Ali Budesh: "Tell this to Imran bhai. This department belongs to him, Eid Gul bhai."

Eid Gul looks toward Imran and is about to say something, but Imran speaks:

Imran: "You'll receive the hare (dollars). Let me reach Dubai, and yes, you need to give me Sami ul Haq's number."

Eid Gul writes down Sami ul Haq's number on a card and hands it to Imran, who keeps the card in his pocket.

Imran: "Thank you for the number. Once I'm in Dubai, I'll provide you with the additional advance. So, when are you planning to go to Dubai?"

Eid Gul: "Tomorrow, I'll leave."

Imran: "So soon? You could stay here for a few more days."

Eid Gul: "I need to go to Lahore from Dubai as well, so I have to leave tomorrow."

Imran: "Alright."

Eid Gul: "Swami ji, now I'd like permission from both of you. And convey my regards to Peter bhai. Let him know that his outlet is splendid."

Ali Budesh: "Zain, absolutely."

After saying this, Eid Gul exits the private hall. Ali Budesh and Imran stay seated. After Eid Gul leaves, Imran takes out a card from his pocket, where Sami ul Haq's number is written, and saves it in his mobile. He sends a message:

"This is my number, Sami ul Haq bhai. Imran."

A reply comes: "Okay, Imran bhai. Sami ul Haq."

After messaging Sami ul Haq, Imran sends a message to Arun's number:

"Arun Bhai, I've met Eid Gul, and he arranged a call with Sami ul Haq. I have his number now. And the boss is in Direct Touch."

A reply comes: "Call in 5 minutes."

After reading Arun's reply, Imran tells Ali Budesh:

Imran: "Swami ji, Arun bhai's message. He'll call in 5 minutes."

Ali Budesh: "Zain, even at this late hour, Arun bhai is active. Despite the strict rules in prison, he manages everything well, I wonder?"

Imran: "Swami ji, he's our brother, colored in the hues of patriotism. He knows that our meeting is ongoing with Eid Gul, so he must have kept his communication device on. And Arun bhai's planning is always foolproof. He hasn't opened the target yet. He's just collecting all the details, and people are actively engaged in their tasks. This time, it's going to be an international game at a high level. That's how I perceive it."

Ali Budesh: "Zain, Arun bhai is no less than an army."

Just then, Imran's phone rings.

Imran: "Hello, bhaiya."

Arun: "Hello, how are you, Imran? And keep your phone on hands-free so that Swami ji can listen to what I say."

Imran switches to hands-free mode and speaks:

Imran: "Yes, bhaiya, I met Eid Gul. He's an expert in all sorts of explosions. You understood what I meant, right?"

Arun: "I see. So, even cars?"

Imran: "Yes, bhaiya, cars too."

Arun: "Alright, stay in touch with him. And what else is happening? Quickly tell me. I can't keep the communication device on for too long. So, provide me with all the details as soon as possible."

Imran: "Bhaiya, Eid Gul was also demanding some funds in advance. I told him that I'll send him from Dubai. He's leaving for Dubai tomorrow and will go to Lahore from there."

Arun: "Now listen to my words very carefully. Tomorrow, you return to Dubai. You need to collect funds. They'll be arriving from Singapore, at an old location. Pick up the notes from there and send as much as I specify to Sami ul Haq. And remember, I've managed crowd funding for this mission with great difficulty. My old Indian patriots abroad are ready for crowdfunding. No one in India is ready to help with the funds. We only show Indian patriotism on Twitter and Facebook. And yes, the 50,000 dollars that Swami ji gave to sami ul haq as an advance, return that to Swami ji right now. I know Swami ji is with you, but I won't be able to talk to him now. I have to close the dabba (mobile). You get to Dubai and I'll tell you what you need to do there after you reach. And remember, stay in direct touch with sami ul Haq. We need a sami ul haq network on any conditions. Bye."

The call disconnects, and Imran tells Ali Budesh:

Imran: "Swami ji, I have your 50,000 dollars with me. Arrange for someone to pick it up from the guest house now. Because I need to leave for Dubai tomorrow. You've heard everything on the call anyway."

Ali Budesh: "Zain, alright, I'll inform Peter, he'll collect it. I should also leave now, it's quite late."

Imran: "Okay, Swami ji."

Ali Budesh calls the waiter over and instructs him to fetch Peter. Peter

Paul David comes over to Ali Budesh and sits on the chair next to him.

Ali Budesh: “Peter bhai, you go with Imran bhai. He will give you something, collect it and then send it to me. I should leave now, it’s getting quite late.”

Peter Paul David: “Okay, boss.”

Imran: “Peter bhai, let’s go, we need to leave now. I also have to arrange the tickets.”

The three of them get up and walk out of the hotel. Ali Budesh gets into his car and heads home, while Peter Paul David takes Imran in his car to the guest house.

****

Chapter 2
PLANNING

While contemplating Ali Budesh and Eid Gul's meeting in Bahrain and suspicions regarding Arun's intentions, Imran finally decided to book a flight ticket from Bahrain's airport for a 9 AM flight to Dubai. Around 1.5 hours later, he arrived at the airport and immediately called the old location in Dubai as per Arun's instructions to collect money. He received a response that the task would be done after 2 PM. Imran sent this message to Arun via mobile, but it wasn't delivered. Imran realized that the communication channel is off now, so he decided to wait and took a taxi from the airport. Upon reaching his accommodation in Dubai, he freshened up and contacted his informants in Nepal and Bangladesh who worked for Imran. He gathered information about the local situation and tasks, which was his daily routine. This practice made his informants always feel under his scrutiny. Imran was quite satisfied with their performance and the recent tasks they had completed. Following Imran's directions and Arun's planning, these informants were responsible for the assassination of Jamim Shah in Kathmandu, Nepal, in 2010. Jamim Shah was involved in smuggling counterfeit Indian currency from Nepal to India, severely destabilizing India's economy, and the ISI of Pakistan was behind it. In more explicit terms, it could be said that Jamim was working for the ISI. This incident gained significant coverage in print and electronic media at that time. In fact, Jamim Shah was a media tycoon in Nepal, using his channels and cable networks to spread deceptive news against India, tarnishing India's image. His assassination was extensively covered by electronic and print media, to the extent that even the Nepalese government sought UN intervention in the case. Several other gangsters also claimed responsibility for his killing. But in reality this action was also carried out based on Arun's instructions to Imran.

Imran instructed his boys to keep an eye on Jamim Shah's residence in Kathmandu. He himself got involved in this task as well. Near Jamim Shah's house was a dental hospital, adjacent to which was a multi-storey hotel. Imran had booked a room in this hotel that had a window overlooking Jamim's house. On the other side, one of his informants from his group would visit the dental hospital for medical treatment, accompanied by his associate. Through this setup, they monitored Jamim Shah's daily activities from both sides. After a while, Imran had a complete understanding of when Jamim Shah left his house, where he went, how much time he spent, and so on. He shared all the details of this reconnaissance with Arun. Keeping a close watch, on February 7, 2010, in front of the French Embassy in Kathmandu, Imran shooters shot Jamim Shah dead. Meanwhile, Imran stood near the French Embassy, smoking a cigarette, observing the entire scene. Coincidentally, the CCTV camera placed outside the French Embassy wasn't functioning that day, which made it impossible to identify the assassin.

Imran represented Arun's hands and feet, while Ali Budesh represented his face. Interacting with the media was Ali Budesh' responsibility, whereas Imran's role was to create chaos.

After speaking with his boys, around 1:30 PM, Imran left his home and headed towards the "old location."

The "old location" refers to Dubai's Bur Dubai. Bur Dubai was given a codename "Purani Jagah" (old place). Bur Dubai used to be the old city before New Dubai emerged. In this Bur Dubai, there are approximately 500 hawala operators. Imran had to collect money from one such hawala operator to whom funds had been sent from Singapore to Dubai.

Imran reached Old Dubai (Bur Dubai) by taxi and collected the money from the hawala operator. Once again, he checked his mobile message box to see if Arun had received the message or not. Thankfully, the message had been delivered. Imran immediately called Arun, but despite the phone ringing, there was no reply. He tried again, but the outcome was the same as before. Frustrated, Imran hailed a taxi and headed back home. Within a few minutes, his phone started ringing incessantly. On the other side, Arun was calling to take a report from Imran.

Imran: Hello, Bhaiya (brother).

Arun: Hey Imran, you know how difficult it is for me to operate here. And you've called twice already. When I find the opportunity, I'll call myself. Remember that for the future.

Imran: Bhaiya, I called to provide the update and for further instructions.

Arun: What's the update?

Imran: Bhaiya, I've collected the money from the old place.

Arun: Now do one thing, directly send 20,000 to Hare (dollars) Sami ul Haq. And before that, talk to him. Also, tell him that we'll need him urgently in Lahore. Another thing, find a Pakistani who can work for us in Lahore. Whether he's a criminal, most wanted, or a businessman, it doesn't matter. He just needs to be willing to work for us. Make sure he doesn't go separate from us; we need to have a hold on him. In fact, we need to keep him for someone's surveillance in Lahore. I'll let you know whose surveillance later. First, find the right person for the job.

Imran: Ok , Bhaiya (brother). Bhaiya, I was thinking, if someone needs money, we can give them the money and use their vulnerability to get our work done. Through this, they won't distance themselves from us.

Arun: You have to see this. I'm here,You are My eyes. Imran, I am like Dhritarashtra of this modern Mahabharata, and you're like Sanjay. What you see is what I'll be able to see. Keep your eyes open. Find a Pakistani guy who can go to Lahore. We'll talk about the rest later.

As Arun finished speaking, he disconnected the call. Imran, in the taxi, was pondering how to find someone suitable for their work in Lahore. The taxi reached his home. Imran was engrossed in thoughts about finding the right person for their job. He decided to take a moment to relax. He thought he would talk to Sami ul Haq in the evening and send him the money.

In the evening, Imran woke up and began contemplating how to find someone for their job in Lahore. Surveillance was not an easy task, and finding the right person was crucial. Imran decided to call Sami ul Haq.

Sami ul Haq: Hello.

Imran: Sami ul Haq, I need to send Hare (dollars) to you.

Sami ul Haq: Alright, how many?

Imran: 20,000 Hare (dollars).

Sami ul Haq: I'll send you the address. You can deliver it there.

Imran: Sami ul Haq, you can send the address. But I also want to tell you that we'll need your help in Lahore very soon. Prepare your network there.

Sami ul Haq: Don't worry about that. Eid Gul will set up everything in Lahore. I'm sending you the address.

The call disconnects, and along with the disconnection, Imran receives a message on his mobile phone. The message contains the address of a travel agent. The travel agent's location is close to Imran's home. Imran walks over to the travel agent's location and deposits 20,000 Hare (dollars) with him. From the travel agent's place, Imran goes to a Pakistani dance bar, thinking that he might strike up conversations with people there and maybe someone might have information or clues related to his purpose. Despite spending 2-3 hours and money at the dance bar, he returns empty-handed. While walking, he realizes that maintaining communication with the gatekeeper could be beneficial. This was a clever move from his past experiences where a gatekeeper's help had led to the attempted assassination of the Pakistani terrorist Zakir ur Rahman Lakhvi while he was imprisoned. It was also part of Arun's planning. However, even the relationship with the gatekeeper turned out to be an unsuccessful endeavor.

Twenty days pass. Imran spends these 20 days in continuous meetings from morning till night. He meets new people and reconnects with some of his old acquaintances. Those old contacts had previously assisted Imran. But this time, even Imran's old assets couldn't provide much help. Imran was troubled by the thought of how to respond to Arun. During these 20 days, Imran didn't receive any calls from Arun. Imran takes the initiative to send a message, informing Arun that the search is ongoing. Today, he was supposed to meet an old contact named Rashid. This meeting was scheduled to take place at the ground floor coffee shop of Dubai Mall. Imran reaches Dubai Mall on time and meets Rashid at the coffee shop.

Imran: Salam, Rashid bhai.

Rashid: Waalekum Salam, Imran bhai.

Imran: You didn't have to wait, did you?

Rashid: No, not at all.

While talking to Rashid, Imran notices a person who has accompanied Rashid. Rashid understands that Imran wants to know about that person.

Rashid: Imran bhai, meet Sahim Sheikh. He has his specialties, and he holds considerable influence in Pakistan.

Imran: What kind of influence, Rashid bhai?

Rashid: Oh, it's about manpower. Sahim is an expert in pigeon racing.

(Note: "Pigeon racing" refers to the illegal practice of sending laborers abroad without proper visas or papers. Many laborers from Pakistan and Bangladesh go to the Middle East for work through such illegal means. There are many operators who facilitate this process.)

Imran: Very well, then this seems quite useful.

Rashid: Absolutely, brother. Imran bhai, you may need anyone for any work at any time. Just let Sahim bhai know. Isn't that right, Sahim bhai?

Sahim Sheikh, sitting calmly, responded with a smile.

Sahim Sheikh: Give me a chance to serve, Huzoor.

Imran: It's good that we met & you came with Rashid bhai today. I want to know how you manage to transport people from one place to another.

Sahim Sheikh: Look, brother, I'm all about money. I don't care about what someone does or what they have done in the past. My job is to transport them from one place to another. What they do there is none of my concern. I charge someone 50,000 rupees to bring them from one place to another. That's all I care about. Is that alright?

Imran: What if the person you transported, without proper papers, turns out to be a criminal?

Sahim Sheikh: Imran bhai, whether they are criminals or not, I'm only concerned with money.

Imran: You seem to be focused on your work. I need a person who is Pakistani and can work for us in Pakistan.

Sahim Sheikh: What kind of work?

Imran: Nothing special, just to keep an eye out.

Sahim Sheikh: Keep an eye on what?

Imran: You just mentioned that you're all about money, and there's no need for you to know.

Sahim Sheikh: Hehehe. I provide you with someone who suits your work.

Rashid, who had been listening to the conversation, chimes in.

Rashid: Sahim bhai, give your number to Imran bhai and stay in direct touch. Imran bhai is into big things. Because of Imran Bhai Our pockets are always full.

Sahim Sheikh writes down his number on a piece of paper and hands it to Imran. Imran puts the piece of paper in his pocket.

Rashid: Imran bhai, now we must leave, there's more work to do.

As Sahim stands up from his chair, Imran says to Sahim:

Imran: I hope that you will find someone soon for my work.

Sahim Sheikh: By tomorrow, I will provide you with the pigeon (man) . You need to see whether it can handle a long flight or not. Call me tomorrow evening after 6 to discuss.

After this conversation, Sameem Sheikh and Rashid leave the coffee shop, while Imran remains seated there, sipping his coffee. Suddenly, Imran's phone rings, and it's a call from Arun.

Arun: How are you doing, Imran, Whats the update?

Imran: Bhaiya I am still working on it

Arun: It's been 20 days, and you haven't achieved anything yet. I haven't called or messaged you for the past 20 days. If I don't call you today, you won't have any updates. Hurry up with this task, and remember that the person we need should be a bit smart, active. We don't want someone who…

Imran: Yes, yes, I understand, bhaiya. Don't worry, I'll do something soon. I've talked to some people, and we should have some results by tomorrow.

Arun: Alright.

Arun disconnected the call, and Imran was tangled in thoughts about how to arrange someone for Arun's task who could excel in it. The challenge was that he didn't even know the target. Who the target was and what they were like, he only received a clue that a $10 million reward was offered by the American government for whoever it was. The matter was complicated, so the person had to be capable as well. While pondering over these thoughts, Imran hoped for positive results from his conversation with Sahim Sheikh the next evening.

The next day, Imran spent his entire day restless, wondering whether Sahim Sheikh would find a suitable person for his task or not. As time passed, Imran approached Ali Budesh, Sami ul Haq, Eid Gul, and even the guy from Nepal, one by one, to inquire about their well-being. Finally, as the clock struck 6 in the evening, Imran started dialing Sahim Sheikh's provided number.

Imran: Hello, Sheikh Sahib, this is Imran speaking.

Sahim Sheikh: Imran bhai, Salam. I was just thinking about you. Let's meet tonight at 8 o'clock at Bur Dubai Hotel.

Imran: Sheikh Sahib, come to York Hotel in Bur Dubai. My table is always reserved there. So, let's meet there at 8 o'clock.

Sahim Sheikh: Alright, Imran bhai. I'll be there at 8 in the evening.

Imran: 8 o'clock in evening. Khuda Hafiz.

Sahim Sheikh: Khuda Hafiz.

Imran places his phone aside, lights a cigarette, and turns on the TV to watch the news from India. His home is just about 10 minutes away from York Hotel, and there's still around 2 hours left until 8 o'clock. Imran watches the news until 7:15, then heads to the bathroom to freshen up. After his shower, he gets ready for the precious meeting and puts $2000 from the money he collected yesterday into his pocket. He then sets off for Hotel York.

He stops at the entrance of Hotel York and takes out a cigarette. As he's about to light it, a hand touches his shoulder, and Imran turns around to see Sahim Sheikh standing behind him. They greet each other and enter Hotel York together. Imran was a frequent visitor to Hotel York, which is why he received VIP treatment there. A waiter guides him to a cabin-like area with a laid-out table, leading Imran there.

Imran: Sheikh Sahib, did you come empty-handed? Didn't you bring the pigeon (man) to showcase its flight?
Sahim Sheikh: The pigeon is on the way.

Imran: Hmmm... What would you like to drink?

Sahim Sheikh: can drink anything, but it must be Scotch.

Imran signals the waiter with his eyes and orders Black & White Scotch for himself and Sahim. As they place their order, Imran spots a.6-foot-tall man approaching their table. His arrival catches Imran's attention.

The newcomer's gaze meets Sahim Sheikh's, and Sahim Sheikh nods, signaling him to take a seat. The newcomer is wearing a Pathani suit that seems like it hasn't been cleaned in a long time. His hair is disheveled, and his hands look as though he has just emerged from a coal mine. Imran is momentarily disappointed.

Sahim Sheikh: Imran, meet Javed. He's from Dara Pakistan and has some unique skills.

Javed: Salam, Bhai.

Imran: Salam. What do you do here in Dubai?

Javed: Bhai, I can do anything. Be it killing, lifting, or driving a car – I can do it all. Just tell me the job.

Imran, after seeing Javed and hearing his words, is initially disappointed, thinking that this person might not be suitable for the task at hand. Arun needs someone smart and attentive, not a 6-foot tall rustic.

Imran: Let's discuss the job. But first, have something to eat; you're our guest.

Saying this, Imran signals the waiter and tells Sahim Sheikh to step outside for a moment.

Imran and Sahim Sheikh leave the cabin-like place and step outside the hotel. Once outside, Imran addresses Sahim Sheikh.

Imran: Sheikh Sahib, this person is of no use to me. He doesn't seem fit for the purpose I have in mind. What I need is someone a bit educated, smart, and capable of using their brain. Along with that, they should have daring. Even a cheater, but Javed won't work.

Sahim Sheikh: I understand your point now, Imran Bhai. You need someone specific for your task. Imran Bhai, people like that are usually found in jail, those who have been imprisoned for fraud, cheating, and extra daring. We'll have to find them there. My employee once told me about a

Pakistani who could be just the person you're looking for. However, he's currently in jail. If someone could get him out of jail, he'd be willing to do anything for money. Give me some time; I'll find out.

Imran: Alright, Sheikh Sahib. Just remember, the pigeon must be strong, and time is running out.

Saying this, Imran crushes the remaining cigarette with his foot and heads back home. The next day, Imran's sleep is disrupted by the ringing of his phone. He answers and sees that the caller is Sahim Sheikh.

Sahim Sheikh: Salam, Imran Bhai.

Imran: Salam, Sheikh Sahib. It's early in the morning; I hope everything is okay?

Sahim Sheikh: Everything is fine. I just wanted to let you know that I've gathered information about the pigeon I mentioned yesterday. Canyou meet me at 1 PM…

Imran: Your service is quite fast... 1 PM at Hotel York.

Sahim Sheikh: Alright, Imran Bhai.

Imran checks his watch; it's 10 AM. He places his phone on the side table when he receives a call from Ali Badesh.

Ali Badesh: salam alekum, Imran Bhai.

Imran: Salam, Swami Ji, how are you?

Ali Badesh: I'm well, by the grace of Allah... Everything's fine in Dubai. How's work going?

Imran: Work is going well. Bhayia (Arun) is satisfied with what he asked for.

Ali Badesh: That's good. Keep it up, and if you need anything from my side, let me know.

Imran: Certainly, Swami Ji.

Ali Badesh: By the way, I'll be a bit busy for the next day or two. As I told you earlier, I'm in the process of registering a new house. So, next time when you come to Bahrain please stay at my place instead of the guesthouse.

Imran: Of course, Ali Bhai.

Ali Badesh: Alright, that's all I wanted to inform you. Have a good day.

Imran places the phone back on the table and goes back to sleep to complete his remaining three hours of sleep.

Exactly at 1 PM, Imran arrives at Hotel York and finds Sahim Sheikh already waiting for him in the hotel's lobby area. They exchange greetings.

Imran: What's the news, Sheikh Sahab?

Sahim Sheikh: The news is good, Imran Bhai. The man you were looking for is in Dubai Central Jail, involved in fraud and cheating cases. He's a Pakistani and has been in Dubai jail for the past 2-3 years. He doesn't have the money to get himself out.

Imran: What case landed him in jail?

Sahim Sheikh: He got caught in a cheating case... But I can't say much about it. You should meet him in person in jail. If he seems suitable, keep him with you and use him for your pigeon. Talking more about him right now wouldn't be appropriate. I've arranged a meeting time. Its at 1:30 PM, and the jail is about 30-40 minutes from here.

Imran: Alright, let's finish this beer and get going. No need to delay.

Imran and Sahim Sheikh both arrive at the jail on schedule. Their meeting with the person Sahim Sheikh referred to takes place in a room at the jail, and they are introduced through Sahim Sheikh's pigeon. Sahim Sheikh: Imran Bhai, meet Naved. Naved, this is Imran Bhai. He will get you released from prison, but just do as he says. You need to work for him if you wanted to be out.

Naved greets Imran, and Imran responds with a "Wa-Alaikum-Salaam."

Naved's full name was Naved Akhtar Khan. He was originally from Faisalabad, Pakistan, and worked as a contractor in Dubai. Alongside his contracting work, Naved also worked as a real estate agent. Naved had given a bounced cheque to one of his suppliers, which resulted in him being sent to jail. He didn't have the money to pay the penalty and get out of jail. Naved was a sharp-minded individual, willing to do anything to get out of jail. He was married, and his wife and children were going through tough times in Pakistan. Naved was unable to send any money home from jail, and this was the reason he was ready to do whatever it took to get out.

Imran asks Naved a few questions and then leaves the room. As he exits, Naved looks at Sahim Sheikh and asks if they will really gets him out or not. Sahim Sheikh looks at Imran for an answer, but Imran leaves without saying anything. Sahim Sheikh follows Imran, and Naved watches them both as they go.

Imran exits the jail and lights a cigarette, contemplating that the pigeon has potential. He decides to take action. The rest of the conversation can wait until tomorrow. Imran hails a taxi and heads home. Inside the taxi, he sends a message to Arun: "Please call." However, the message fails to deliver. Imran keeps his phone on the side and gazes out the taxi window, observing the sights of Dubai. The taxi eventually stops in front of his house. As Imran exits the taxi, Arun's call finally comes in.

Arun: Tell me, what's the situation?

Imran: Bhaiya, I found the pigeon. He's in jail, and he seems to be exactly as you described - attentive and sharp. We just need to do our part from our side.

Arun: Is he from Pakistan?

Imran: Yes, Bhaiya.

Arun: What was he doing in Dubai?

Imran: He used to work as a contractor. He took construction contracts and also worked as a real estate agent. But now, he's in jail.

Arun: Why is he in jail?

Imran: He's in jail for a bounced cheque case.

Arun: A real estate agent. This could work. I'll tell you what to do tomorrow.

Imran: Yes, bhaiya.

Arun hangs up the phone, and Imran takes a deep breath, feeling the results of his hard work over the past 20-25 days.

The next day, Imran receives a call.

Arun: Imran, assign the task of getting the pigeon out to Sami ul Haq. Whatever expenses are involved, you provide them to Sami ul Haq. I don't want anyone to find out that we're responsible for getting Naved out. If anyone manages to extract information from Naved tomorrow about who got him out, Naved should mention Sami ul Haq, meaning TTP. I don't want our name to be associated with such a big mission. Let TTP's name be the one circulating. Imran, from now on, you'll only communicate with

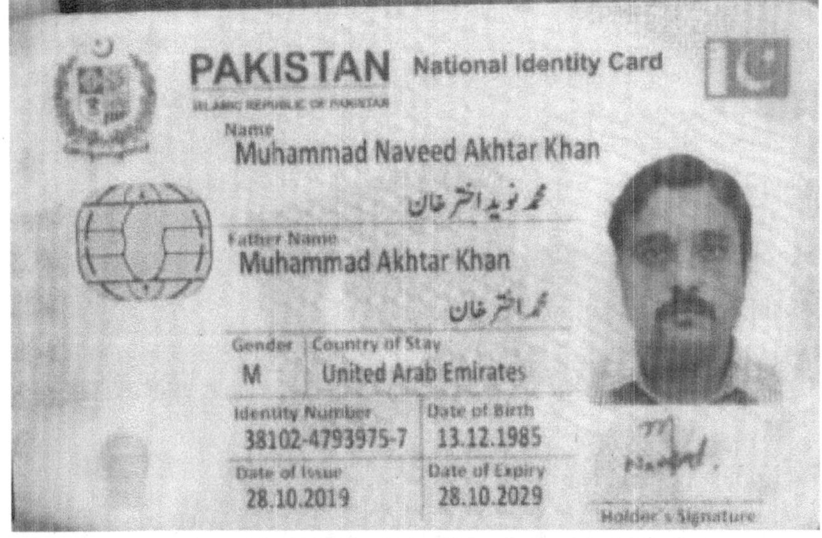

Naved Akhtar Khan Photo ID

Sami ul Haq; the rest of the work will be handled by him. Keep this matter confidential.

Imran: Understood, sir.

Arun: I've also collected some funds through crowdfunding. Retrieve them from the old place, and whenever Sami ul Haq asks for money, provide it to him. I'll let you know what to do when the pigeon is out of jail. For now, that's all.

Imran: Yes, sir.

After Arun hangs up, Imran immediately calls Sami ul Haq.

Imran: Sami ul Bhai, I have a task for you.

Sami ul Haq: Tell me, I'm at your service.

Imran: There's a guy in Dubai jail, Naved. We need to get him out of there as soon as possible. And once he's out, we'll discuss the next steps. Just remember, the condition for getting him out is that he must work for our surveillance when he's out. Only if he's willing to work for us should he be released.

Sami ul Haq: Alright, Imran Bhai. Give me some time to figure this out, and I'll update you.

After receiving instructions from Imran, Sami ul Haq starts preparing to get Naved out of jail. He contacts his Dubai associate, Haider, and provides him with details about Naved. Haider learns that Naved's pending amount in the cheque bounce case is 35,000 UAE Dirhams. If Naved can deposit this amount, along with the penalty, he can be released immediately. Sami ul Haq instructs his man, Haider, to meet Naved in jail and make it clear that he needs to follow instructions upon release. Haider take appointment at Dubai jail and Haider reaches jail to meet Naved.

Haider: Naved, arrangements for your penalty have been made. In return for that, you will have to work for the people who are doing all this for you.

Naved: What kind of work will I have to do?

Haider: Now, since they are getting you out, you'll have to work in exchange. If you don't want to work for us, then you can stay in jail. Over here, you'll be in jail, and there, your wife and children will starve.

Naved: I want to get out, but I'm still curious about what the work is all about. Will I get anything in return for the work?

Haider: You'll have to keep an eye on someone. You'll work for TTP. Have you heard of TTP?

Naved: Who doesn't know about TTP? If TTP is involved, I also want some money in return for the work.

Haider: You'll have to talk to TTP's boss about the money. My job is to get you out. If you don't want to come out of jail, stay there.

Naved: Are you angry? I just want to know if I'll get something or not. Who wants to stay in jail? I want a lump sum amount, so I can settle my wife and children outside Pakistan, and in return, you can keep getting the work done. Just a lump sum of 10 crores.

Haider: I'll talk to them.

Haider leaves the jail and calls Sami ul Haq to inform him that Naved is demanding 10 crore rupees to get his family safely out of Pakistan.

Sami ul Haq: Tell him we'll give him 10 crores. What's the harm in saying it? He'll work for that 10 crore. Our job will be done, and yes, also mention that the expenses for surveillance will be provided separately.

Haider: You're doing a great job, Bhai. It seems you've understood that he's greedy.

Sami ul Haq: Whoever asks for 10 crores, consider them greedy. Greedy people only work for greed. Get him out and send him to Lahore. Khua Hafiz.

Haider: Khuda Hafiz.

Haider returns to the jail and informs Naved.

Haider: I've conveyed your message to top leaders, and they have agreed to the 10 crore rupees. However, you will receive the money only after the surveillance work is completed. Additionally, any expenses related to surveillance will be given separately. Now, Naved, I will arrange for you to be released from here.

After finishing his conversation, Haider starts to leave the place. Haider did not wait to see Naved reaction as he knew that Naved would agree to everything according to his wishes. Just then, Naved calls out to Haider loudly.

Naved: Inshallah, I'm ready Bhai. Okay?

Haider, upon hearing Naved's affirmative response, smiles and exits the jail. He promptly calls Sami ul Haq to deliver the good news that they have gained control of the situation. Sami ul Haq informs Haider that the necessary amount of money will be provided to him by tomorrow in order to secure Naved's release. After this,Sami ul Haq contacts Imran.

Sami ul Haq: Imran, your task is complete. Naved will be out soon; he's just demanding 10 crores for his work. I've already said yes for the funds. The rest, you'll have to handle and send it to me in exchange for Naved's release.

Imran: Alright, you'll receive the remaining funds.

After speaking with Sami ul Haq, Imran calls Arun, and coincidentally, Arun's phone is active.

Imran: Bhaiya, Sami ul Haq are demanding 10 crores to get Naved out, and Naved is asking for this amount in exchange for surveillance work. Sami ul Haq has already promised for the funds to Naved.

Arun: Filling up the funds won't be a problem. I know Sami ul Haq has only promised to fund Naved, but he won't give it. However, what we can do is that we can let him take the money from us. Our main concern is Imran this time; the target is very important. Even a small mistake can jeopardize the entire mission. Also, remember, TTP is crucial for us. Without TTP, we can't do anything in Lahore. Now, listen carefully. As soon as Naved is out of jail, arrange for his transfer to Lahore. Tell him to set up his residence near the Tauheed Mosque, Johar Town area. When he finds a place to stay in that area, let me know. After that, I will guide you on what to do next.

Imran: Okay, bhaiya.

Arun: We'll discuss the rest later.

After speaking to Imran, Arun starts thinkig very seriously about the next stage of planning. There are several issues - what if Naved, Sami-ul-Haq's man, couldn't carry out the task with the same precision that Sami -ul-Haq had expected? Then the mission fails. The TTP, which plays a crucial role in executing the mission in Lahore - if they object to anything , then again, the mission fails.

I never reveal the full plan to anyone, because the next move exists only in my mind. God forbid, if any of my men are caught by the ISI - even then, they won't be able to get anything out of him.

The entire plan is only in my head. If everything goes right, we succed. If not, years of effort will go to waste, and my desire to do something meaningful for the nation will remain just a wish in my heart.

Anyway, let's seee what happens next and most importantly - even if this planning fails, there's still another plan in my mind. It will just take more time.

After his conversation with Arun, Imran makes a call to Sami ul Haq.

Imran: I'll send you 20,000 Hare (Dollars) and will have it delivered to the same travel agency you mentioned before. As soon as Naved is out, you can send him to Lahore, instructing him to find a house near the Toheed Mosque in the Johar Town area. Once he's settled there, I will guide you on what to do next.

Sami ul Haq: I have already told my guy to get Naved out soon.

After completing the paperwork and paying the penalty of 35,000 dirhams, it took 5 days to get Naved out of jail. As soon as Naved is released from prison, he meets Haider outside the jail.

Haider: Welcome, Naved. Now you'll be flying high. But before you soar, I'll arrange for you to have a chat with the boss from TTP. Let's get in the car.

While getting into the car, Haider calls Sami ul Haq and informs him that Naved has been released from jail and is with him. Sami ul Haq suggests that Naved should talk to him directly. Haider hands his mobile phone to Naved, who hesitates but takes the call.

Naved: Salam, Bhai and thank you for getting me out. This guy will be your servant for life. Thanks for helping me escape this hellhole.

Sami ul Haq: You're welcome. Now you are our man, and we take care of our people. You need to go to Lahore. Find a house near the Touheed Mosque in Johar Town Lahore. Haider will provide you with some money for your Lahore expenses, and he'll arrange your flight to Lahore. I will instruct you on what to do once you're in Lahore. Take my number from Haider and get a local SIM when you arrive in Lahore. Message me when you do.

Naved: As you say.

Afterward, with a sigh of relief, Naved hands the phone back to Haider. Meanwhile, Haider talks to Sami ul Haq and nods in satisfaction.

Haider takes Naved to a hotel asks him to take some rest & at 10 PM Haider came to meet Naved in Hotel, he provides Naved with tickets, some Pakistani rupees in an envelope for expenses, and a phone. The envelope also contains a Sami ul Haq phone number written on a piece of paper. Naved puts the money, phone, and tickets in his pocket, and a smile of happiness and contentment appears on his face. Haider tells him to take a taxi to the airport tomorrow and stay in touch with Sami ul Haq once he reaches Lahore.

The next day, as soon as Naved arrives in Lahore, his first task is to get a local SIM card. His Local Mobile Sim Number was +92-3018349999 He messages Sami ul Haq with the SIM number, and then he calls his wife and children. He informs his wife that he has managed to escape from Dubai and is now in Pakistan. He tells her that he plans to start a business in Pakistan and will soon call her and the children to join him.

While talking to his family, Naved receives a call from Sami ul Haq.

Sami ul Haq: Naved, shift to a hotel for now and start looking for a house near Touheed Mosque in Johar Town area. This should be done quickly, within 2-4 days, and keep reporting to me.

Naved wanted to say something, but Sami ul Haq disconnects the call without listening to him and Sami Ul Haq calls Imran.

Sami ul Haq: Imran, the pigeon has landed. What's the next step?

Imran: We'll discuss the next steps later. First, let him settle down at his new place.

Sami ul Haq: Alright, but we need some more funds.

Imran: You'll get the funds.

Sami ul Haq: Thank you.

Imran disconnects without further discussion and contacts Arun.

Imran: Arun Bhaiya, Naved has arrived in Lahore. Sami ul Haq is demanding more funds.

Arun: Alright, alright. Give him 70,000 Hare (dollars) this time. When Naved finds a house, make sure he sends the location map and the house number to Sami ul Haq. Tell Sami ul haq that Naved needs to set up a real estate business at that location. Naved was already involved in real estate in Dubai, so he should start a real estate business in Lahore as well. For that, arrange an office for him near Touheed Mosque with personal parking. The office area should be exclusively for Naved's office, with no one else sharing the building. This office will be crucial for our work. I'm sending 70,000 hare(dollars) for all these tasks.

After speaking with Arun, Imran makes a call to pass on the instructions provided by Arun to Sami ul Haq. Imran tells Sami ul Haq that Naved needs to have an office along with his residence, and before finalizing the residence, he should send the house number and map to that location in advance. The office for Naved should be spacious and located in the same area. It should have personal parking. Imran also tells Sami ul Haq that he's sending 70,000 hare (dollars) for all these tasks.

Sami ul Haq listens carefully to all the instructions and forward the same instructions to Naved but he did not tell Naved about the $70000. Naved contacts a local real estate agent to find a residence. The agent informs Naved that finding a house in the Touheed Mosque area is very difficult, but he will try his best and starts looking for a house in the area.

The agent takes Naved to several flats in that area, but Naved rejects all of them outright. The issue was that Naved was well aware that TTP was behind all this operation, and it was their money. So why not enjoy some privacy and comfort? Therefore, Naved tells the agent to find a bungalow for him in the same area. The agent asks Naved to wait for a few days. After two days, the agent takes Naved to a bungalow in the Touheed Mosque area. Naved really likes this bungalow. The house number was 123E, and it was right in front of Touheed Mosque. Naved downloads the number and location map of the bungalow from zameen.com and sends it to Sami ul Haq. Sami ul Haq forwards all these details to Imran. Imran then forwards all this information to the main character in this chain, Arun.

Arun just responds with 'OK' and sends a message to Imran. He tells Imran that he will thoroughly investigate the map and details of the area for the next few days. He wants to make sure that Naved's residence is in a strategically useful location. After a few days, Arun calls Imran.

Arun: Imran, what Naved and his agent have accomplished in arranging his residence is truly commendable. I must say, for the success of our operation, it feels like even the divine is on our side. Whether you're Imran or Ali Badesh or Sami ul Haq from TTP, all of you have executed my plan without knowing what I'm ultimately up to. Let me shock you, Imran. My target is none other than Hafiz Saeed.

Imran: (Surprised) What are you saying, Bhaiya? Hafiz Saeed?

Arun: Yes, Imran. Hafiz Saeed, who orchestrates numerous attacks in India every year. How many lives are lost in those attacks, you know? You surely remember the 26/11 Mumbai attacks because our media covered it extensively. However, many attacks go unnoticed by the media. Now, it's time to teach Hafiz Saeed a lesson. For this entire operation, we need a substantial amount of money. I'm arranging crowdfunding through my sources abroad to gather as much as possible. Imran, remember, the name of our prey should not reach Sami ul Haq under any circumstances. First, complete the rental agreement for the house legally. Once Naved has shifted there, we will inform Sami ul Haq of the next steps.

Imran is taken aback by the revelation that their target is Hafiz Saeed.

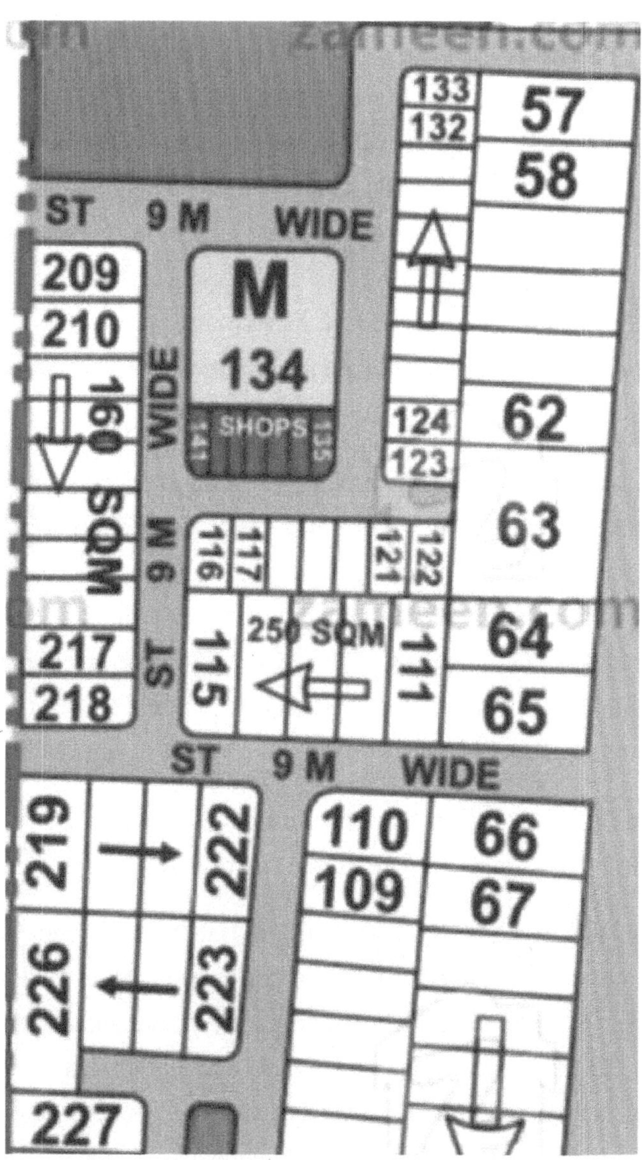

House Map From Zameen.com

Imran: Yes Arun Bhaiya.,

Hafiz Saeed is India's most wanted international terrorist. He is also the mastermind behind the Mumbai attacks on November 26. Hafiz Saeed has been sentenced in Pakistan, but he has never actually gone to jail. Instead, he used to run his madrasa in Lahore and acquired all the houses near the Touheed Mosque. The Touheed Mosque in Johar Town Lahore has become Hafiz Saeed's safehouse. The U.S. had put a $10 million reward on Hafiz Saeed. But even after the reward was announced, Hafiz Saeed was never targeted, unlike how the U.S. targeted Osama bin Laden in Pakistan.

After receiving instructions from Arun, Imran calls Sami ul Haq and tells him to inform Naved to complete all the formalities for acquiring the house as soon as possible. Sami ul Haq gives Naved the green signal to take the house he saw. Naved is happy about getting a bungalow to live in, and TTP is providing him with the money. Naved tells the real estate broker that he can take the bungalow. The real estate broker prepares the rental agreement, setting the monthly rent at PKR 45,000 and a security deposit of PKR 90,000. Naved sends a copy of the agreement to Sami ul Haq.

Sami ul Haq confirms the agreement for Naved's Lahore residence and sends the agreement copy to Imran & Imran sends copy to Arun.

Arun instructs Imran to tell Sami ul Haq to send a spy camera to Naved, and when Naved receives the spy camera, Sami ul Haq should inform him of the target's identity using code names such as Chachajaan (paternal uncle), Maamojaan (maternal uncle), Abbujan (father), or Fufajaan (maternal uncle). This way, even if the phone is compromised, nobody will know who Chachajaan, Maamojaan, Abbujan, or Fufajaan really is. Imran immedialtely relays all the orders given by Arun to Sami-ul-Haq. However , he noes not disclose who needs to be monitored. Sami-ul-Haq promises Imran that he will send a spy camera to Naved as soon as possible. A few days later, Sami-ul-Haq informs Imran over the phone that Naved has recieved the spy camera. Hearing this, Imran finally reveals the secret and begins to speak.

Imran: "Sami Bhai the one Naved needs to keep an eye on is Hafiz Saeed, who lives very close to Naved's bungalow."

Sami ul Haq: "What are you saying Imran bhai? Hafiz Saeed?"

Imran: "Yes, and please tell Naved that whenever he sends any videos or messages for surveillance, he should add the code names Chachajaan, Maamojaan, Fufajaan, Abbujaan, or he should just say jaan word at the end. If phone compromises occur, no one should find out who Chachajaan, Maamojaan, Fufajaan, Abbujaan, or this jaan person is."

Sami ul Haq: "If we had known earlier that the surveillance was on Hafiz Saeed, we could have demanded more."

Imran: "You are still demanding more"

Sami ul Haq: "This time, make sure you send some more & extra funds."

Imran: "It will be arranged."

Sami ul Haq then calls Naved and informs him about the surveillance target being Hafiz Saeed. Naved requests some advance payment upon hearing Hafiz Saeed's name. Sami ul Haq realizes that Naved is now bargaining harder since he knows the target. He agrees to provide some advance payment and asks Naved to find an office quickly.

Naved starts to make acquaintances with people near the Tauheed Mosque and also begins searching for an office. Naved lived in Dubai and worked in the real estate business, so he informed everyone that he wanted to start a real estate business here as well. His experience in real estate was proving useful in his work, and through his communication skills, he quickly established his identity among the people living near the Tauheed Mosque.

Arun instructs Imran to tell sami ul haq to instruct Naved to create a map himself. The map should include the location of Naved's house, the location of the Tauheed Mosque, and where Chachajaan comes and goes from. Imran sends this message to sami ul haq , and sami ul haq instructs Naved to create a map by hand.

Naved surveys the entire area, and once he understands the entire area, he prepares a map himself. He records a video on the handmade map and sends it to sami ul haq , explaining all the details in the video. Whatever Naved had sent to Sami-ul-Haq via video is presented here exactly as it was.

Naved: Sir, this is the service road, all right. On the side of this service road, we have the main road, okay. On the left side, there's Faisal Bank. They come from here, and there's a checkpoint here. The police car is parked here, and there are two gunmen. Then, further inside, this is Chachajan's house. This is the gate, and here's the generator. Chacha comes from here to go to the mosque, and this is the Madrasa with 2 basements. Then, this is the second road. Here, there are two police officers standing, and there's a barrier ahead. There's a checkpoint here. Here, three police officers are standing, and this is the public park, all right. The point is that I can stand at the gate or on the balcony of my bungalow and keep a close watch on the Madrasa, Mosque, and Chachajan's house's exits.

Naved sends a voice-over video of the detailed map he created with his own hands to sami ul haq . He sends the same video to Imran, and Imran forwards that video to Arun. Arun watches the video and understands the area. Once he comprehends the area through the map, Arun calls Imran.

Arun: Imran, has the spy camera reached Naved or not?

Imran: Yes, it should have been reached by now.

Arun: Find out if it has reached. Tell Naved to make a video of the area and show where the generator is kept, where the police guards and barriers are, and whether he has taken the office or not. If he hasn't taken

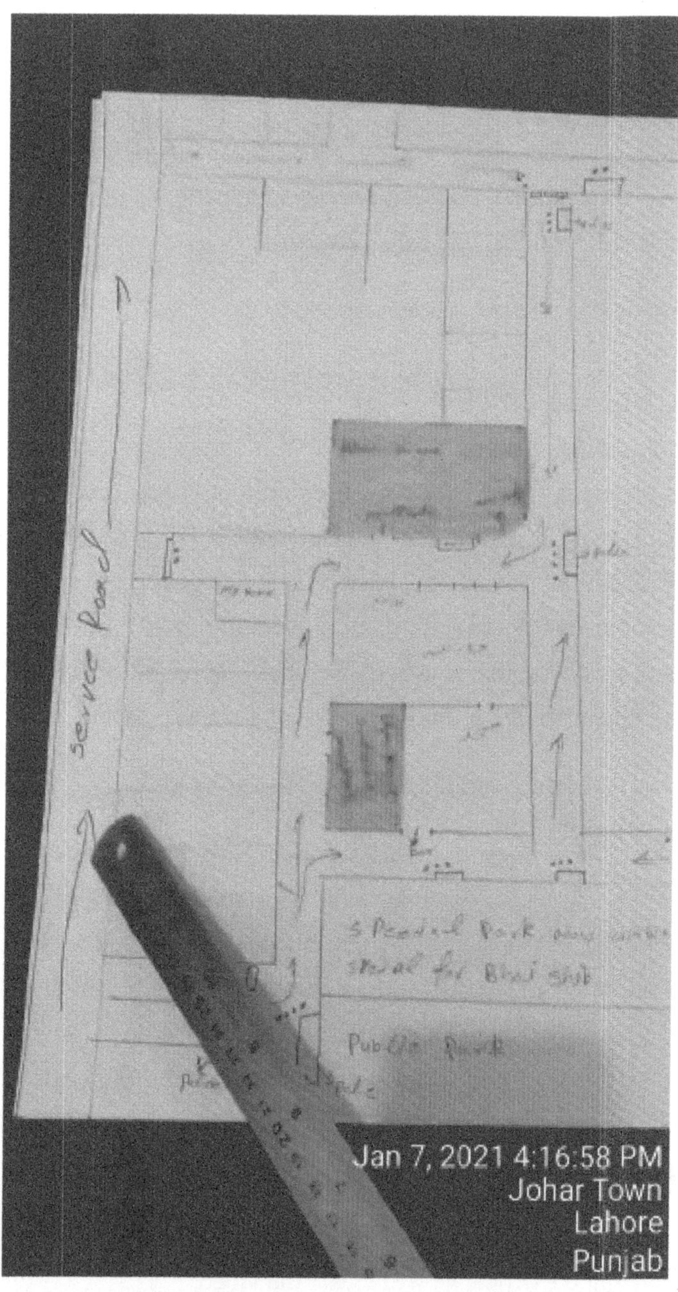

Naved - Handmade Map - Video Grab

the office, make it clear that we'll provide the further payment once the office is secured.

Imran: Okay, I'll talk to him right away.

Imran calls Sami ul Haq and provides him with the instructions given by Arun. Then, Sami ul Haq calls Naved.

Sami ul Haq: Naved, what happened to the office?

Naved: I'm still looking for the office. Alright, I'll find it soon.

Sami ul Haq: Find the office quickly, otherwise, I won't provide the advance payment. Search for the office promptly, and there's one more task. Use the spy camera I gave you to make a video of the entire area, showing where the barriers are, where the police guards are stationed, and how many personal guards are there at the entry gate. Also, locate where the generator is kept; this is crucial. So, make the video and send it to me. And yes, remember again: find the office as soon as possible.

Naved: Alright, Sami ul Bhai.

Sami ul Haq doesn't discuss further. Naved understood that if he wants money, he has to work for TTP. This condition is why he is freely moving around in Pakistan today. Even if he thinks about backing out of TTP's work now, TTP will eliminate him and his family. He finds himself stuck in a situation where he can neither spit out the bone nor swallow it. Naved then thinks, "Well, what's wrong with doing these kinds of videos and keeping an eye on Chachajan? After that, I'll get a hefty sum. Then, I can start a new life in another country."

Naved now decides that his first attempt will be to find the office, and after finalizing the office, he will create the video.

Naved's entire effort is now focused on finding a suitable building for the office. Through a property agent, he was shown a building that would serve as an office, located a near Faisal Bank, on the main road and a short distance from Tauheed Mosque. To get to the office building from his home, he had to pass by the barricading in front of Hafiz Saeed's house, which was right next to Tauheed Mosque. Naved liked the office building, which was like a bungalow, with a local restaurant on one side and another bungalow on the other side. This bungalow-style office building had only one gate for entry and exit, with no sharing. There was also ample parking space in the building.

Naved sent photos and information about the office to Sami ul Haq, who, in turn, forwarded it to Imran and Imran forwarded to Arun. Arun conducted a detailed study of the office building and provided his recommendation for using the building for the office.

Arun: Imran, the office building is suitable. Tell Sami ul Haq to convert this bungalow into a furnished real estate agent office. Keep some staff there, and make sure Naved spends at least 2-3 days in the office each week. Imran, if this bungalow is left vacant after renting it, there's a risk that it will come to others' attention, which could put Naved at risk. Naved can use this as his real estate dealing office; he has experience in real estate from Dubai. He will work efficiently in this office. Also, Sami ul Haq willl request the setup expenses for the office, which you'll send to him through Swami Ji. Don't send the money directly, let it go through Swami Ji. Whatever money Sami ul Haq demands, send it to Swami Ji, and Sami ul Haq will collect it from Swami Ji. Once Naved completes the office setup, we'll discuss what to do next. Imran, tell Sami ul Haq that we still haven't received the video showing the location of the generator, police, personal guards, and barricading. Naved should send that video as soon as possible.

Imran: Yes, bhaiya, I'll convey all this information.

Naved Office Building From Outside

Naved Office Building From Outside

Imran calls Sami ul Haq and informs him to rent the office and instructs Naved to transform the building into an office setup. He also mentions that Naved hasn't sent the video yet. Sami ul Haq listens to Imran's entire conversation and assures him that everything will be sorted, and the video will be received soon. When Sami ul Haq asks Imran for money, Imran suggests that the money should be collected by Sami ul Haq from Swami Ji. After talking to Imran, Sami ul Haq calls Naved and inquires about the video.

Naved: Bhai, I was looking for the office, so I haven't made the video.

Sami ul Haq: Now that the office is finalized, go ahead and rent the building. Set up the agreement quickly. As soon as you get the office, start your real estate business in it. You should spend 2-3 days a week in this office; this work should be done quickly. I will send you the money for the expenses involved in this work.

Naved: Alright, Sami ul Haq Bhai, I understand.

After speaking to Sami ul Haq, Naved brings the real estate broker to his home to prepare all the paperwork for renting the building. During tea and coffee, all the documents are signed. Naved leaves the broker there and, under the pretext of freshening up for a minute, goes to his bedroom to attach his spy camera to his golf cap. This spy camera supports GPS tagging, and it had the special feature that it recorded and highlighted the location of objects and targets during recording.

Leaving the broker and continuing the conversation while walking outside the bungalow, Naved goes to talk to the personal security personnel stationed at Chachajaan's house, near the generator. He also initiates a conversation with the police officers stationed at the barricades further ahead. In this way, he manages to execute all the tasks that Sami ul Haq had instructed him to do. Along with this, he records a 3-minute and 14-second video of the local area, which he sends to Sami ul Haq. Finally, the lengthy network of video sharing and reporting that Arun had set up pays off. If Naved is ever caught, he won't be traced back as the main master planner because he received orders from Sami ul Haq through intermediaries in Turkey. Naved only knew that he was working for the TTP and that all of TTP's leaders were far from Pakistan's reach.

Arun, after watching the video, understands the security and layout of the area. After fully comprehending the situation, he calls Imran.

Arun: Imran, now give Naved instructions to shift with his family to that location and increase communication with Chachajaan's people. He should get closer to the people living in the nearby bungalows and the children. Also, keep recording videos to see what activities are taking place. Additionally, ensure that Chachajaan prayers in the Tauheed Mosque should be recorded. Build connections with the people in the mosque and madrasa. Naved needs to do all of this right away, inform Sami ul Haq.

Imran: Yes, bhaiya, I'm going to tell him now.

Imran provides all the instructions given by Sami ul Haq to Naved, who then follows these directives.

Naved sets up the office in the building he rented and brings his entire family from Faisalabad to Lahore. When his family arrives in Lahore, Naved creates a video proof of their arrival and sends it to Sami ul Haq. He continuously records videos using the spy camera and sends them to Sami ul Haq. In these videos, Naved shows Hafiz Saeed's house and the mosque as soon as he leaves his home. He also captures the activities happening around his house in these videos.

Naved Checking His Spy Camera - Video Grab

Generator Outside Hafiz Saeed House - Video Grab

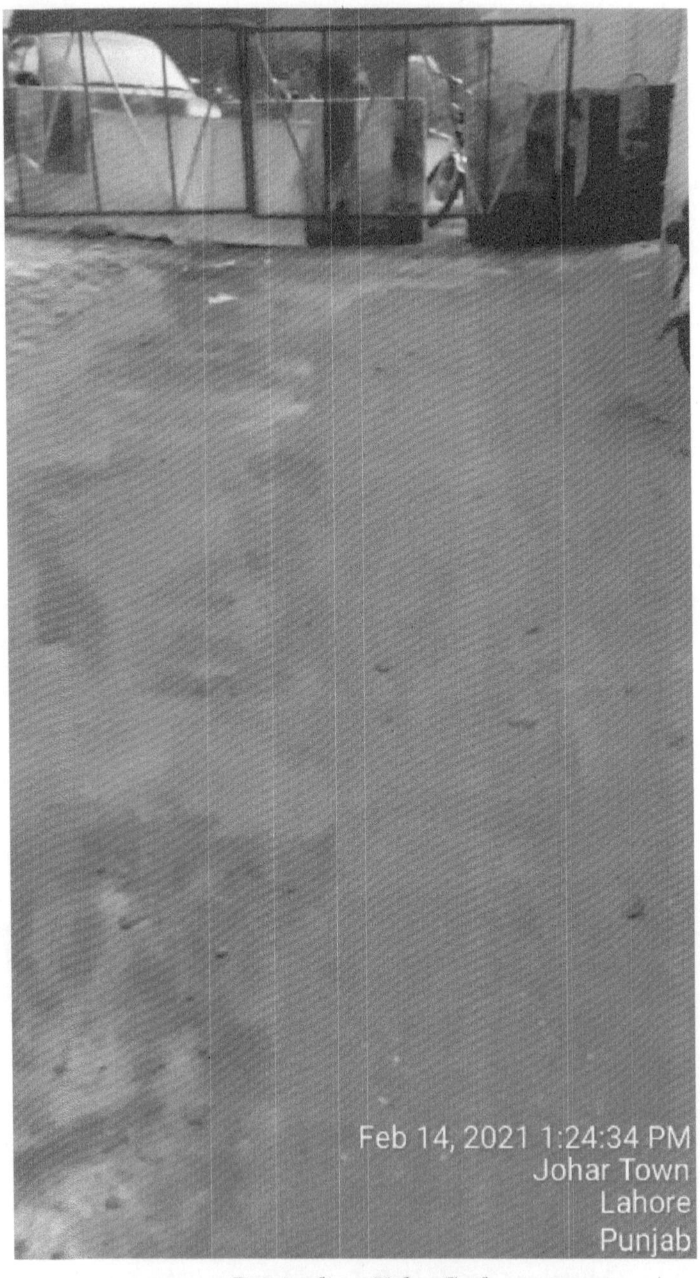

Barricading- Video Grab

Generator Outside Hafiz Saeed House - Video Grab

Hafiz Saeed House - Video Grab

Hafiz Saeed House View From Naved House - Video Grab

Hafiz Saeed Personal Guard - Video Grab

Naved had reduced his phone conversations with Sami ul Haq and was now communicating through voice messages. The primary reason for using voice messages was that Naved had established good connections with the local people. Both Naved and Sami ul Haq were keen on ensuring that no one overhears their conversations.

During this time, Naved had infiltrated deeply into the area, including Hafiz Saeed's security and staff. He often invited Hafiz Saeed's people to his home, and he also started visiting the homes of Hafiz Saeed's people. Naved's goal was to capture even a glimpse of Hafiz Saeed through his spy camera. However, Hafiz Saeed's security was so tight that before entering the mosque or Hafiz Saeed's house, everyone would undergo thorough checks. Naved couldn't risk getting caught with the spy camera, which could lead to dire consequences.

Naved had established a friendship with Gul Khan, one of Hafiz Saeed's key associates. Gul Khan took Naved to Hafiz Saeed's house, under the pretext of showing construction work. After this meeting, Naved sent a voice message to Sami ul Haq explaining the details of his visit.

Naved: Assalamualaikum, sir. How are you, my dear brother? I met Gul Khan after a long time, following a lot of struggle. So, I have had a meeting with the person in charge of the work, who is working for them. We sat for about 10 minutes, had tea, and so on, but the people at the reception took away our watches, mobile phones, and pens.

Afterwards, I was introduced to Chachajaan, but he isn't feeling well. He uses a stick to walk. Apart from that, he's fine, sitting and talking. I've reached this far, but directly doing something further, like taking pictures and sending them to you, is currently not feasible. I'm still trying. If I manage to get pictures or videos, I will send them to you. Alright.

Naved's message reaches Sami ul Haq, Sami who ultimately relays the information to Imran and from it reaches to Arun. Arun listens to the message and joyfully calls Imran.

Arun: What I wanted, Imran, has happened.

Imran: I don't understand,Bhaiya????

Arun: It has been confirmed that Chachajaan is indeed in that same house, not in any jail. The Pakistani government kept claiming that Hafiz Saeed was in jail. But in reality, he was living comfortably at his home. The doubt has been cleared. Now, you tell Naved to try to get closer to Chachajaan in any way possible. Find out when Chachajaan comes and goes. I mean, when he leaves or returns to his home. This needs to happen quickly.

Imran: I understand, bhaiya.

Pakistan has always denied that Hafiz Saeed was living at home and insisted that he was serving his sentence in jail. But in reality, he was enjoying a luxurious life at his residence.

Imran gives Sami ul Haq all the instructions over the call, and Sami ul Haq relays the same instructions to Naved.

Naved continues his efforts but doesn't succeed in getting closer to Hafiz Saeed. The pressure from Sami ul Haq is mounting, and when Naved feels the pressure, he sends a voice message to Sami ul Haq.

Naved: "Assalam Alaikum, bhaijaan. I want to let you know that I'm not going anywhere, and I've put my work on hold, including our home business. So, every morning, I freshen up and take the kids to the balcony. I take them out into the street, engage in conversations with people. This is what I'm trying right now. InshaAllah, within 2-3 days, I'll report back to you, God willing. I'll also send you some pictures or videos of Abbujaan. Please be patient; it will work out, God willing. You had mentioned earlier that we need to follow up carefully. If you had told me earlier that we need to act quickly and forcefully, I would have devised some plan. Right now, I'm focused on building relationships with those people. I have developed good relationships with all of them, so everything should be fine with a bit

Naved With His Family - Video Grab

Naved in His Car - Video Grab

of patience. InshaAllah, I will only bring good news. May Allah do good."

After receiving Naved's voice message, Sami ul Haq gets Arun Instructions through Imran, Arun Instruction that they should allow Naved to continue his work without applying any pressure. For several days, there is no specific information coming from Naved. He continues sending videos from the spy camera, but they all show the same location, security measures, and barricades. However, Naved succeeds in building relationships with key individuals, including Hafiz Saeed's security guards, police guards, madrasa staff, and residents of the Tauheed Mosque area. Naved often invites them to his house, fostering connections. He also starts attending prayers at the Tauheed Mosque. One day, Sami ul Haq receives a voice message from Naved. Naved: "Assalamualaikum, Bhaijaan. All is well. Today, I had a meeting with Chachajaan, and it went well. I even prayed with him."

Naved's message was a game-changer for Sami ul Haq, Imran, and Arun. No one had ever imagined that Naved would read prayers with Hafiz Saeed. Naved had become a perfect asset, providing information beyond anyone's expectations. Sami ul Haq has been sending money to Naved, and the money is provided by Imran, and if the mission succeeded, a $10 million bounty was also at stake. Both money and reputation were on the line in this mission. After receiving information about Naved praying with Hafiz Saeed, Arun calls Imran. Arun: "Imran, Naved has started praying with Hafiz Saeed. Now, it's confirmed that Hafiz Saeed is permanently staying there, and Naved has gained everyone's trust. Now, with Naved, we can arrange entry for anyone. Our job has become much easier. The Day of Judgment is coming soon for Hafiz Saeed. I'll instruct you on how to proceed. Wait until tomorrow, and then inform Sami ul Haq."

Imran: "Ji Bhaiya. I'll wait for your call."

Army Commando in Hafiz Saeed Security - Video Grab

Chapter 3
EXECUTION

In 2018, the mission began, and by 2020, two years of hard work had paid off for Arun and his team as they successfully tracked Hafiz Saeed. However, at the beginning of 2020, the COVID-19 pandemic started wreaking havoc. But, at that time, the impact of COVID-19 was limited to China and Europe, and the Indian subcontinent had not been significantly affected. Amidst news of the coronavirus, Naved sent a voice message to his handler, Sami ul Haq.

Naved: "Salam bhai, I'm doing my job well. According to the promise, you need to give me share of the 10 crores. I need it to set up my business., I'm continuing to do your work."

Sami ul Haq responded to this voice message with a simple "Okay." Meanwhile, Imran received a call from Arun.

Arun: Imran, first, you need to instruct Sami ul Haq to obtain the exact location tag for Hafiz Saeed's house, which is in front of the mosque and the madrasa. Sami ul Haq should send the precise location tag via Google Maps using GPS. Additionally, Also tell Sami ul Haq that Naved should purchase two identical cars - the same make, model, color, and accessories. Everything about them should be identical, right down to the seat covers. If one car has a scratch, the other car should have the exact same scratch. Whether Naved assembles them himself or someone else does, both cars must be identical. Do you understand? Also, one car should remain covered in the office parking lot, while the other car should be used by Naved to go to his office and home. I will provide further instructions shortly.

Imran: Yes, bhaiya. I have received a message from Sami ul Haq. In fact, some others from his team wanted me to meet them here in Dubai. Sami ul Haq is becoming demanding he is asking for more funds. Arun: How much money have you delivered to Sami ul Haq so far?

Imran: Bhaiya, I've given him around 500000 dollars.

Arun: You've given quite a bit of money, and you must continue to do so; otherwise, it could raise suspicion. I'll collect more money from our friends; let's see who can contribute. But sending money is essential. How much money do you have right now?

Imran: I have around 1 lakh in cash.

Arun: Imran, you should talk to Swamiji; I had kept 5 crores aside for another mission a long time ago. However, that mission didn't materialize, and the money needed to be returned. But now, it seems like we'll have to use some of that money for this mission. Ask Swamiji for 10 lakhs. We'll discuss the rest later. I'm switching off the dabba (mobile); I'll call tomorrow; checking is ongoing. I need to keep it hidden. Imran disconnects the call and thinks about the mission. He calls Swamiji, alias Ali Budesh, and asks for 10 lakhs, which he receives in Dubai on the same day. Imran then transfers the money to sami ul haq , following Arun's instructions.

sami ul haq sends a substantial amount of money to Naved. Afterward, Naved sends the first GPS location of Hafiz Saeed's house. Following this, he purchases two identical cars, Toyota Corolla of the same color, but these are second-hand cars bought in Lahore. One reason for buying second-hand cars was to avoid drawing attention, as purchasing two brand-new luxury cars simultaneously would raise suspicions. After a lot of effort, both cars are modified to look identical, from gear handles to seat covers. Even the tires are replaced to match those on the first car. Finally, both cars are intentionally scratched to look the same. The cars now look indistinguishable from each other.

After completing all the work on the cars, Naved sends a message to Sami ul Haq, informing him that the tasks he assigned are complete. Sami ul Haq relays this message to Imran. However, when Imran tries to message Arun, the message fails to deliver. After some time, Arun's calls, and Imran receives the call.

Arun: Imran, there's one more thing to do with the cars Naved bought. Get extra heavy shock absorbers installed in both cars because if there's too much weight, they won't handle it well. Also, tell Sami ul Haq to keep a Mujahideen ready. Sami ul Haq mentioned an RDX expert; what's his name?

Imran, listening calmly, responds:it's Eid Gul...

Arun: Yes, Eid Gul... Tell Sami ul Haq to put Eid Gul in the field and introduce him to Naved over the phone. We Need Eid Gul RDX Expertises in one of the Naved Car.

Imran: Ok Bhaiya,and I have sent the money to Sami ul Haq.

Arun: You handle the accounts. I'm only concerned with the work. I just want this task to be completed as soon as possible. The coronavirus from China is wreaking havoc worldwide, and China is under lockdown. I hope the rest of the world doesn't follow suit. So, if a lockdown happens, this task should be completed before that. Tell Naved to ensure that our designated car is to be planted somewhere with a driver. I'll provide details later.

Imran: By the way, what's the plan? Leaving a car won't be enough. Are we supposed to send a sniper in the car?

Arun: Imran, don't worry about what to send. Just do as I say. Imran, sounding anxious, disconnects the call after speaking with Arun. He then calls Sami ul Haq.

Imran: Salam, Sami ul bhai.

Sami ul Haq: Waalekum Salam.

Imran: Sami ul bhai, arrange for a mujahideen for our mission. And yes, it's time to activate Eid Gul, the RDX expert as well.

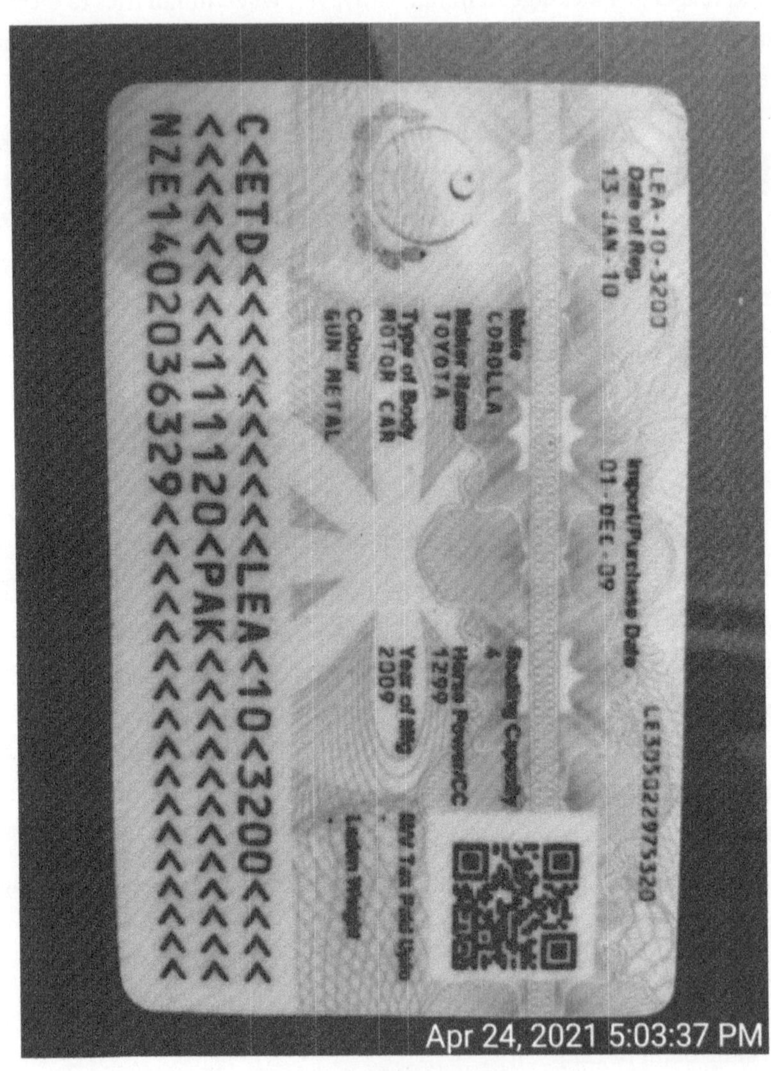

Car Registration

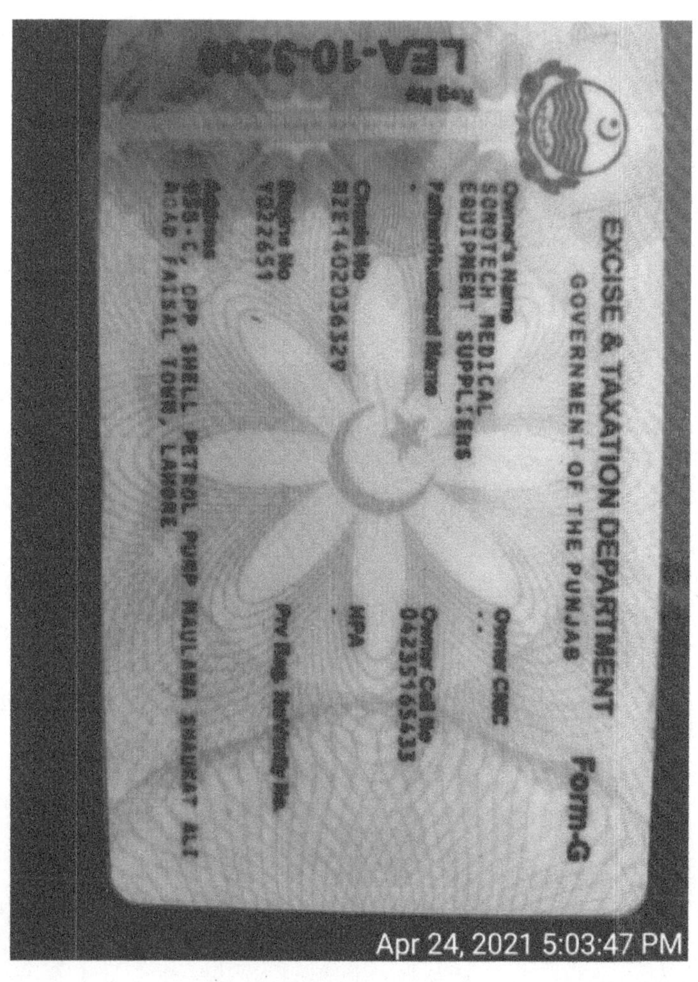

EXCISE & TAXATION DEPARTMENT
GOVERNMENT OF THE PUNJAB
Form-G

Reg No
LEA-10-320

Owner's Name
SORDTECH MEDICAL
EQUIPMENT SUPPLIERS

Owner CNIC
:

Father/Husband Name
.

Chassis No
NZE1402036329

Owner Cell No
04235165433

Engine No
1027651

MPA

Prv Reg No/Vehicle No.

Address
95B-C, OPP SHELL PETROL PUMP MAULANA SHAUKAT ALI
ROAD FAISAL TOWN, LAHORE

Car Registration

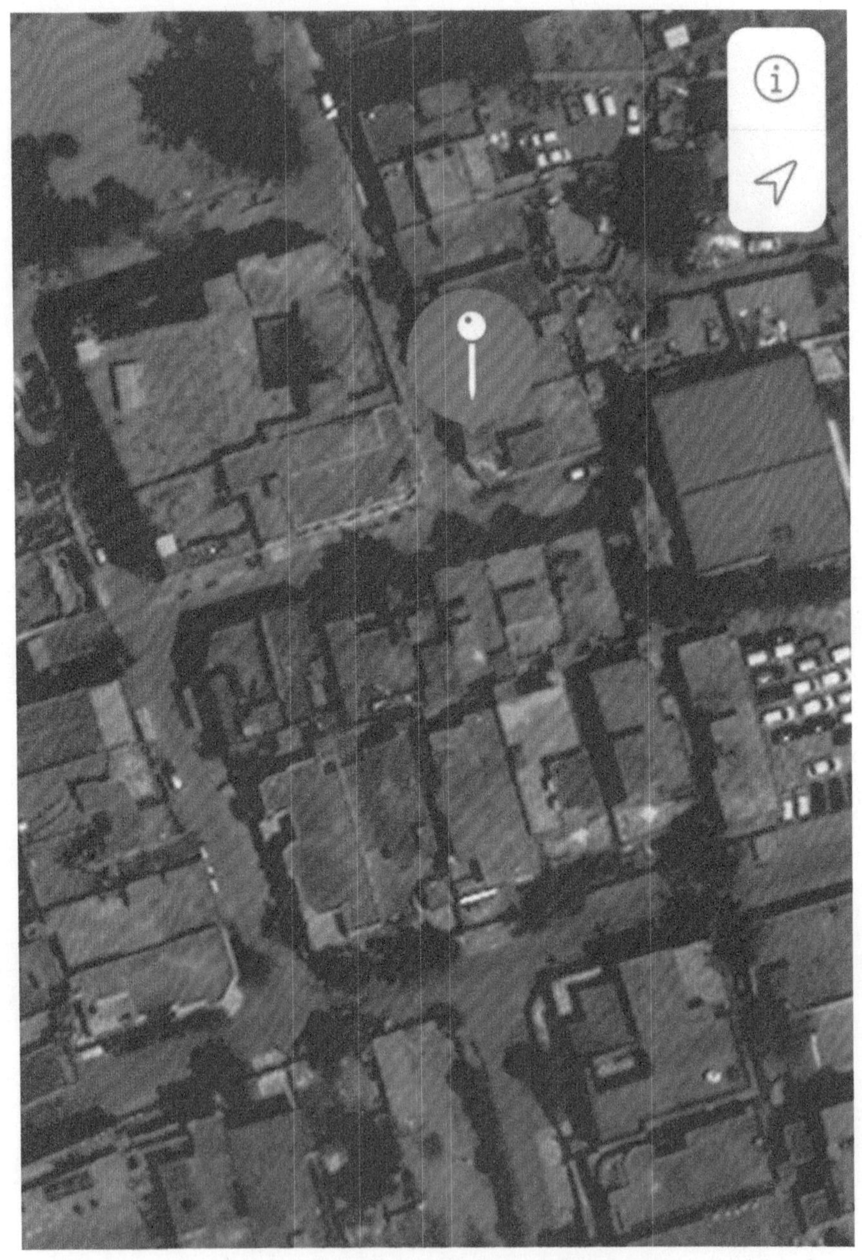

GPS Tag - Hafiz Saeed House

GPS Tag - Hafiz Saeed House

Two Same Car Parked Inside Naved Office

Sami ul Haq: The arrangement for the mujahideen will be made, brother. And as for Eid Gul, he's not under your direct command, but he's fully active in Lahore.

Imran: Excellent. Sami ul bhai, please instruct Naved to start using the two cars he has.

Imran disconnects the call, imagining the upcoming events with great intensity. On the other hand, Eid Gul is in Lahore and begins to establish contact with Naved. He starts visiting Naved's office regularly.

Meanwhile, in the Indian subcontinent, observing the havoc caused by the coronavirus, Arun realizes the urgency of the mission. He contacts Imran to provide him with further instructions.

Arun: Imran, before anything else, tell Sami ul Haq to inform Naved to start using the cars for commuting between home and the office, frequently switching between them. Remember, the number plates on both cars should remain the same. We need to find out if there's any noticeable difference in the cars while they pass through the barricades in front of Chachajaan's house on the route from home to the office. Security guards stationed there shouldn't detect any variation between the two cars. Do you understand? Both cars should be seen coming and going, and this routine should continue for at least 10-15 days. After that, I'll let you know what to do next. What about Eid Gul?

Imran: Ji Bhaiya, Eid Gul is with Naved.

Arun: For a few days, separate Eid Gul from Naved. Eid Gul and Naved shouldn't be seen together for a while.

Imran familiarizes Sami ul Haq with Arun's instructions. Following Arun's guidance, Imran keeps Eid Gul away from Naved as instructed. Naved starts using both cars alternatively as per the plan. Both cars were identical, and no security guard noticed any difference between the two cars. Naved can now travel in and out freely, with no specific checks.

Within 15 days, the situation at the barricading in front of Chachajaan's house stabilizes, with Naved's car not being checked anymore. Naved benefits from residing near Hafiz Saeed's house, and his connections with the locals, guards, and police start to pay off. He can now travel in his car without much scrutiny. On the other hand, Naved receives information about the Mujahideen from Sami ul Haq. He was an Afghan Mujahideen. His name was Mohammad Idris, he lived in Turkey.

Arun communicates with Imran to provide further instructions.

Arun: Imran, tell Eid Gul to plant RDX in one of the cars. Make sure there's just enough RDX to ensure that Chachajaan's house and basement are destroyed. My target is only Chachajaan. If too much RDX is used, the people in the vicinity will also be affected, which I don't want. Our fight is against terrorists, not innocent civilians. Pay special attention to ensuring that the RDX is limited to Chachajaan only.

While Arun is delivering these instructions, Arun receives a news alert on his mobile that a lockdown has been imposed, and Pakistan has also initiated a lockdown.

Arun: Imran, check the news, a lockdown is being imposed. We might have to halt our operations as soon as possible. Talk to Sami ul Haq and let me know.

Imran talks to Sami ul Haq, and then Imran learns that a lockdown will begin in Pakistan from March 24, 2020. Sami ul Haq informs him that now Mohammad Idris, the mujahideen coming from Turkey, can't enter Pakistan, and Eid Gul is in Lahore's safehouse, while Naved is at his home. The mission given to Sami ul Haq will have to be postponed due to the lockdown.

Immediately after this, Imran, with a heavy heart, provides all the information to Arun over the phone.

Imran: " Arun Bhai, the lockdown in Pakistan has been confirmed. Now, Mohammad Idris, the mujahideen (suicide bomber) coming from Turkey, can't enter Pakistan. Eid Gul is in Lahore's safehouse, and Naved is at his home."

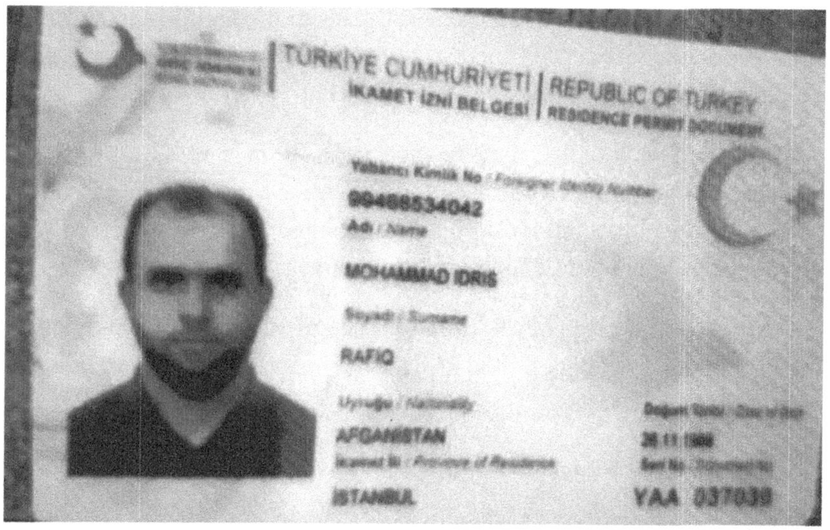

Mujahadeen - Sucide Bomber

Arun: "Now, there's nothing we can do. Two years of hard work seems to be in vain due to this coronavirus. This was the right opportunity to seek revenge for the 26/11 Mumbai attacks. Let's wait and see what happens next when the lockdown is lifted."

The lockdown continues for an extended period, and the plans that had been in progress since 2018 to eliminate Hafiz Saeed now seem to be on hold. Arun, Imran, and Sami ul Haq stay in contact with each other. Even during the lockdown, Naved continues to share information about Hafiz Saeed with Sami ul Haq. But the information gathered about Hafiz Saeed during the lockdown was of no use because he, too, is confined to his home, and Naved, likewise, is confined in his house. Naved shares whatever he can observe from his balcony with Sami ul Haq.

After a few months, they receive news from a news channel that Pakistan will partially lift the lockdown. People will be allowed to leave their homes for essential work, but markets and other activities will not fully reopen. Arun learns about this development from Imran.

Arun: That's great news, Imran! It seems like we're on the path to finally achieving revenge for the 26/11 Mumbai attacks. How are things in Dubai?

Imran: There's a lockdown at night, but some relief during the day.

Arun: I've heard that India will soon resume some flights. As soon as flights are operational, come to India.

Imran: Yes, bhaiya, as you say.

The lockdown went through several phases. In Pakistan, the situation worsened due to the coronavirus. Lockdowns were imposed at various times. Interestingly, the entire year 2020 passed amid lockdowns and precautions. Meanwhile, Naved renewed the rental agreement for his bungalow and extended it for one more year, signing it on 01/12/2020. In December, he also extended the rental agreement for his office for one more year.

In 2021, some countries resumed international flights. Flights started operating from Pakistan as well. The first international flights to resume were to the UAE and the Maldives. Although restrictions were easing, international travel was not fully back to normal. However, Maldives was one of the countries where direct flights from Pakistan were available.

Amidst all this, Arun receives a call from Imran.

Imran: Bhaiya, Pakistan is opening up, and there are special flights from Dubai to India as well.

Arun: Imran, flights have also started from some countries to Pakistan. You should check if Sami ul Haq can send the mujahideen to Pakistan or not. And you should also consider returning to India via the special flights soon.

Imran asks sami ul haq if Mohammad Idris, the mujahideen (suicide bomber) from Turkey, can come to Pakistan. Sami ul Haq informs him that it's still difficult for Idris to come from Turkey, so they need to find a way to execute the plan in Lahore.

Imran shares the information provided by Sami ul Haq with Arun.

Arun: Alright, if the mujahideen can't come to Pakistan, then use Naved. Fit RDX into the car he has, and Naved will take the car to his home. Install a remote blast system in the car because the mujahideen have the capability to detonate themselves with the car & now mujahideen can not come so it's time to use the remote blast system. Make it clear in very strong words that the RDX should only be used to target Chachajaan's house and basement. Using more RDX might harm people nearby, which I don't want.

After receiving instructions from Arun, Imran speaks to Sami ul Haq to pass on Arun's instructions to him. And Sami ul Haq instructs Eid Gul to prepare the car. Eid Gul, who is considered an explosives expert, makes thorough arrangements for RDX and goes to Naved's office to install RDX in the car. From there, he takes the car to his safehouse. Upon reaching the safehouse, Eid Gul fits RDX into the car and also fixes a remote detonator in the car. Due to the heavy shock absorbers installed in the car, even after loading several kilos of RDX, there is no suspicion or indication when the car is seen that it is overloaded. On the other hand, through Sami ul Haq, when Naved learns that he has to plant the car near Hafiz Saeed's house, he becomes worried about the safety of his family and is very concerned about discussing this matter, so he contacts Sami ul Haq on the phone.

BN300535

Rupees 50 — ۵۰ روپیہ

اقرار نامہ معاہدہ کرایہ داری

بحق: محمد فاروق ولد محمد عمر، شناختی کارڈ نمبر 35202-2539815-9

ساکن: مکان نمبر E-123 محلہ ایم اے جوہر ٹاؤن، لاہور (مالک)

منکہ: محمد نوید اختر خان ولد محمد اختر خان، شناختی کارڈ نمبر 38102-4793975-7

ساکن: سرور آباد، بھکر کا رہائشی ہوں جو کہ ایک قطعہ اپر پورشن رقبہ تعدادی سات مرلے (07M) واقع: مکان نمبر E-123 محلہ ایم اے جوہر ٹاؤن، لاہور بر مشتمل دو بیڈ اٹیچڈ باتھ، ٹی وی لاؤنج، کچن، ٹیرس بمعہ چھت وغیرہ معہ تین عدد پنکھے، لائٹس ______ عدد، تین عدد ایگزاسٹ فین بمعہ کنکشن ہائے بجلی، پانی اور سوئی گیس (چالو حالت) ازاں مالک محمد فاروق ولد محمد عمر بحساب کرایہ ماہانہ مبلغ پینتالیس ہزار روپے Rs.45,000/- کرایہ پر حاصل کیا ہے۔ دیگر شرائط کرایہ داری مندرجہ ذیل طے پائی ہیں۔

1) یہ کہ مبلغ نوے ہزار روپے Rs.90,000/- بطور سکیورٹی (قابل واپسی) نقد بشکل کرنسی نوٹ مالک مذکور نے ازاں من مقر وصول کر لیے ہیں۔ جو کہ کرایہ میں ایڈجسٹ نہ ہوں گے۔ 2) یہ کہ من مقر نے ایک ماہ کا ایڈوانس کرایہ ادا کر دیا ہے آئندہ ماہانہ کرایہ ہر انگریزی ماہ کی یکم تاریخ تا پانچ تاریخ تک ماہ بہ ماہ ایڈوانس تا مدت میعاد ادا کرنے کا پابند ہوں گا۔ 3) یہ کہ میعاد معاہدہ کرایہ داری ہذا مورخہ 01-12-2020 سے شروع ہو کر برائے گیارہ ماہ طے پائی ہے جس میں توسیع دونوں فریقین کی باہمی رضامندی سے ممکن ہو گی۔ 4) یہ کہ توسیع کی صورت میں ماہانہ کرایہ میں ہر سال کے بعد 10% کے حساب سے اضافہ ہوا کرے گا۔ 5) یہ کہ بل بجلی علیحدہ بمطابق میٹر جب کہ پانی و سوئی گیس ہر دو ازگرہ خود سے ادا کرنے کا پابند ہوں گا۔ 6) یہ کہ من مقر قبضہ پورشن مذکورہ بالا حوالے مالک مذکور ہی کروں گا کسی دیگر فرد کو شکمی کرایہ دار نہ رکھوں گا اور نہ ہی سب لیٹ (Sub-let) کروں گا۔

العبد   العبد

Rent Agreement

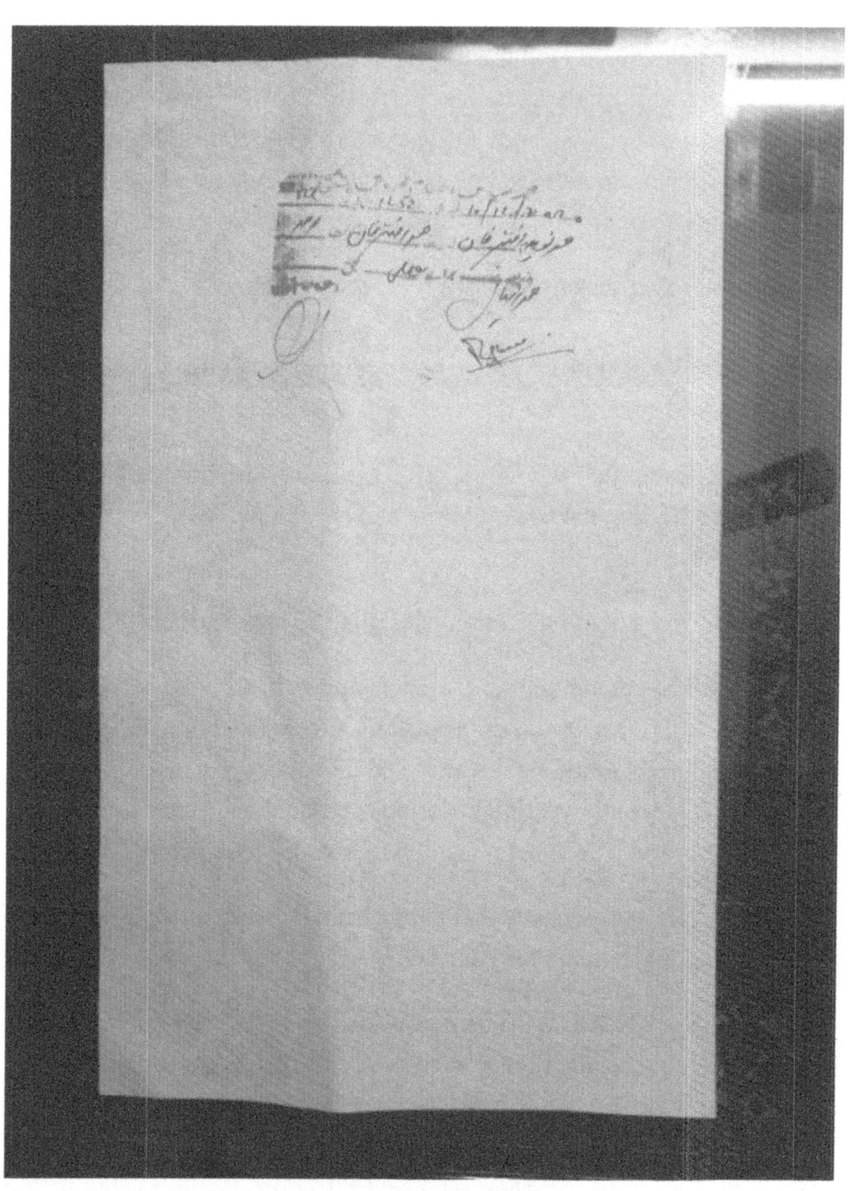

Rent Agreement Back Side

Naved: Bhai ji, I can plant the car, but before that, I need to ensure the safety of my family. Also, besides the 10 crores I asked from you, I'll need to receive extra. My job wasn't just to plant the car, but to keep an eye on everything, and I have done that perfectly, providing you with timely information, whether it's about Chachajaan or the Tauheed Mosque area. Now, it's your turn to increase my compensation and provide an advance. Whether it involves negotiating with your associates to agree to this task.

Sami ul Haq listens carefully to Naved's words and asks him.

Sami ul Haq: Where do you want to take your family? Tell me. I can arrange a house for you there. As for the rest, I will inform you.

Naved: Not in Pakistan or the UAE at all. At this time, only flights to Maldives are leaving Pakistan. For me and my family, Maldives would be a much better option.

Sami ul Haq: Are you planning to settle in Maldives then?

Naved: If there are any other options, please let me know. Traveling during the lockdown has become difficult, and reaching the Maldives during these times would be the most suitable option for my family. So, I need to get to the Maldives as soon as possible, and once I am sure that my family is completely safe there, then I will proceed with planting the car.

Sami ul Haq responds with a heavy heart, saying, "Alright, go to the Maldives and find a home for your family."

After the COVID-19 pandemic in 2020, in 2021, the Maldives was the only country where flights were easily available from Pakistan. So, Naved went to the Maldives from Pakistan without any hassle and started searching for a home for his family. After staying in the Maldives for 7 days, Naved returned to Lahore and sent his entire family to stay with a relative in Pakistan. Upon hearing the news of Naved's return, Sami ul Haq talked to him.

Sami ul Haq: Naved, you're back. It's time to work.

Naved: I am ready to do a job? Alright, but first, you need to give me my 10 crore (rupees). After that, I can proceed with the job. The car I'm driving is the same as the other one, but without my entry, none of those cars can get into the Tauheed Masjid area. So, if you want the car to be planted, you need to give me my 10 crore (rupees) first. I've already shifted my family elsewhere, so now you can't threaten me about my family. You're making big money, and I've taken all the risks. But now, before planting the car, I need to ensure the safety of my family and make them shift to another country and I will finish the job. So, give me my 10 crore (rupees) right now, or forget about the job.

Sami ul Haq was getting increasingly angry, and in his anger, he said to Naved, "Naved, isn't this a bit too much?" But Naved disconnected the phone without listening to Sami ul Haq's entire statement and switched it off. Naved knew very well that the car couldn't be planted in that area without him because both cars were identical. If someone else drove the car there, they would be caught. This was because Naved was the owner of that car, and all the security guards knew him very well.

Sami ul Haq was lost in thought, pondering his next steps. He had already received an advance of 1 million dollars for this job. The entire plan was that explosives would be fitted into Naved's car, and Naved would be given this car. He would then take this car from the office and leave it in front of his house. The mujahideen would then transport the car from Naved's house to Hafiz Saeed's house, near the generator, making it seem like it was stolen. If there was an explosion in the car loaded with explosives, Hafiz Saeed would be finished, whether he was at home or in the mosque. The mujahideen were well aware that they were denoting the car along with themselves, and Naved played a crucial role in this plan. Without his consent, the entire plan was at risk of failing. Due to the lockdown, the mujahideen couldn't enter Pakistan. The explosives Eid Gul had fitted into the car for Naved had to be detonated remotely. Naved's role had become vital, and his cooperation was imperative for the success of the plan.

Naved Outside His Hotel in Maldives

Naved Outside His Hotel in Maldives

Sami ul Haq decided to discuss this matter with Imran, sharing the problem, and Imran passed all this information to Arun. Arun: All of this has gone haywire due to the lockdown. The mujahideen were supposed to detonate Naved's car with him. But now, the mujahideen can't come. So, we are completely dependent on Naved's yes or no. He's demanding 10 crores for this. Although I've already paid a significant amount as an advance to Sami ul Haq, I can't give another 10 crores before the job is done. Moreover, I don't want to step back on this amount at this stage of the operation when success is within reach. Imran, you do whatever it takes to get something out of Sami ul Haq. Threaten him, do whatever you can. But this operation should happen as soon as possible.

Imran talks to Sami ul Haq, successfully intimidating him. Sami ul Haq had understood by now that if this operation didn't go through, his life could be in danger, and these people could ruin his entire network. The one who could pay could also destroy him. In fear, Sami ul Haq decides to talk to Eid Gul.

Sami ul Haq: Eid Gul, the car you prepared with RDX for Naved can't be brought inside now due to the current circumstances. Therefore, you need to find someone who sells old cars and arrange for a car through them. Take the car you buy and fit it with RDX.

Eid Gul: Bhai ji, where am I supposed to get a car out of nowhere? And wasn't Naved supposed to do the car planting job?

Sami ul Haq: Naved is hesitating to do this job, and if this job doesn't get done, the other party will destroy our entire network.

Hearing this, Eid Gul also gets scared and responds fearfully:

Eid Gul: I will try to do something.

On the other side, Sami ul Haq was putting immense pressure on Naved. However, Naved was not willing to undertake this job without being paid and he also learned that Sami ul Haq was planning to proceed with the job through another means. So, to ensure his safety, Naved contacted the local police station in Lahore and revealed everything he knew. The conclusion was that an attack was going to happen on Hafiz Saeed. However, the Lahore police did not pay much attention to this information.

Meanwhile, Eid Gul started looking for someone who could sell an old car for them. Eid Gul needed someone who would provide a car to him without asking too many questions or requiring paperwork. Finding such a car seller was a tough task. After some thought, Eid Gul began scrolling through his phone's contact list. He came across Peter Paul David's number. Eid Gul had met Peter Paul David during his stay in Bahrain, and Peter Paul David had started a second-hand car business. Eid Gul remembered this detail and decided to contact Peter Paul David.

Eid Gul spoke to Peter Paul David, and upon Eid Gul's request, Peter Paul David agreed to provide a car without knowing the purpose it would serve. Sami ul Haq sends 100,000 Pakistani rupees to buy a car from Peter Paul David. Peter Paul David takes the money and delivers an old car to Eid Gul without any paperwork.

Eid Gul informs Sami ul Haq that he has bought an old car & he had placed RDX in the car.

Eid Gul: Bhai, the car has been set up.

Sami ul Haq: Eid Gul, you cannot get the car anywhere near Chachajaan house now; the security there is very tight. Moreover, we are under pressure from the other party. Here's what you should do: plant the car near Chachajaan house, increase the quantity of RDX, and make it big enough to cause extensive damage in the blast radius. Before planting the car, assess the area to determine where Chachajaan could suffer the most damage.

After hearing Sami ul Haq's instructions, Eid Gul begins to scout the main road leading to Tawheed Mosque, especially the route to Hafiz Saeed's house. It becomes evident to him that taking the RDX-laden car to Hafiz Saeed's house from the main road is not feasible. Therefore, Eid Gul starts investigating the back roads.

He eventually identifies a suitable location behind Hafiz Saeed's house, adjacent to the wall, with the house number 113E. Eid Gul devises a plan to park the car with RDX in front of 113E, and from a safe distance, detonate it using a remote control.

After careful consideration, he believes this plan is optimal.

Finally, the day arrives, June 23, 2021. Eid Gul takes the car loaded with 100-125 kilograms of RDX from his safe house, driving cautiously from the safe house to the target area of Johar Town. He ensures to avoid checkpoints or traffic-light areas to avoid drawing any attention.

Eid Gul parks the car near the main gate of 113E, being careful. He then steps out of the car and surveys the surroundings, appearing as if he is trying to locate someone's address. In the meantime, he has the remote control device in his hand, concealed within his pocket.

While walking ahead, another car parked nearby, with his wife, Ayesha Gul, already in the driver's seat. Eid Gul opens the door of the second car and, as he gets in, he discreetly presses the button on the remote control. There's a powerful explosion, and he quickly glances behind. Seeing the task accomplished, he observes Ayesha Gul shifting the car into gear, pressing the gas pedal, and swiftly driving away from the scene.

Behind him, Eid Gul had left devastation. The explosion was so powerful that within minutes, a crowd had gathered there. In the smoke and dust, no one could see anything. House number 113E was completely destroyed, and that's when the police arrived with sirens blaring. They took control of the area and quickly realized that the house behind the one that was destroyed had also suffered significant damage. That house belonged to Hafiz Saeed. As soon as this thought occurred to the police, their attention turned towards Hafiz Saeed's house. Upon reaching there, they found that Hafiz Saeed's security had been compromised. One of his personal guards had died, and several other guards were badly injured. Hafiz Saeed himself had been injured, and most of the windows in his building were shattered. Hafiz Saeed and his security personnel were rushed to the

House Number 113E

hospital in ambulances, and the other injured individuals were also taken to the hospital. Interestingly, despite the blast occurring shortly after Eid Gul's attack, Hafiz Saeed was not seriously harmed, and he was receiving medical treatment in the hospital. Meanwhile, the police and ISI, based on CCTV footage and the information provided earlier by Naved, traced Eid Gul and Ayesha Gul. They arrested both of them. Eid Gul statement provided further information about the entire planning. However, no one knew who the mastermind behind all this was until Peter Paul David was apprehended from Karachi Airport. He was about to board a flight to the UAE. After Peter Paul David's arrest, according to his statement, he revealed the names of Ali Bidesh, Imran (Sanjay Tiwari), and others who had visited his nightclub in Bahrain and how he had met Eid Gul, selling him a second-hand car. In 2022, sami ul haq was also arrested in Turkey. However, Pakistan's government did not acknowledge his arrest in Turkey and presented him as arrested from Baluchistan. sami ul haq , Naved, Eid Gul, Ayesha Gul, and Peter Paul David were all sentenced to death.

Ali Bidesh, who orchestrated the events at Peter Paul David's nightclub and the attack on Hafiz Saeed, Ali Budesh passed away on April 14, 2022, due to a prolonged illness at the Bahrain Army Hospital.

In December 2022, the Pakistani government released a statement and issued a list of involvement. It claimed that this blast had been orchestrated by Arun at the behest of RAW, Arun aka Omprakash Srivastava, also known as Babloo Srivastava, who was serving a life sentence in Bareilly Central Jail.

Now, who will make Pakistan understand that RAW's job is to clandestinely gather information for the country's security and relay that information to the Indian government. Based on this information, the Indian government presents its position in the UN. RAW has never conducted operations of this nature.

Hafiz Saeed is an internationally wanted terrorist, with a $10 million bounty placed on his head by the United States. Many people around the world sought to claim this reward, and some of them formed a group to carry out this task.

It is unknown where Hafiz Saeed is currently located, but he was in his Taheed Mosque, Johar Town, Lahore, residence during the blast. He was injured and underwent treatment in the hospital.

Many consider this attack to be retaliation for the 26/11 Mumbai attacks. It was unimaginable that a person who had been imprisoned for 24-25 years could execute such a significant mission. Planning and organizing from inside a prison, managing funds, gathering people, all without going to the location, and successfully executing the mission, that too from inside a jail, is an astonishing feat.

Ali Budesh Death Condolence Message

Naved in Jail

42 7

peter paul david

جوزف اینتھنی ڈیوڈ

محمود اباد نمبر کراچی، تحصیل وضلع کراچی جنوبی

محمود اباد نمبر کراچی، تحصیل وضلع کراچی جنوبی

1۹

male

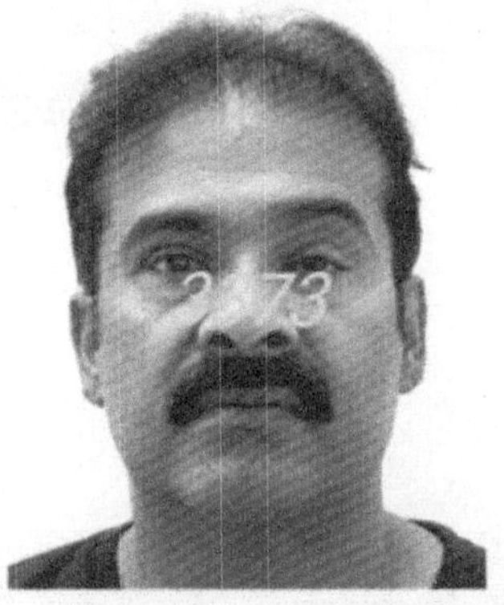

2

Peter Paul David After getting Arrested

Peter Paul David at Karachi Airport -
CCTV Footage Taken By Pakistan Police